The Priestess
and the Slave

The Priestess
and the Slave

Jenny Blackford

HADLEY
RILLE
BOOKS

THE PRIESTESS AND THE SLAVE
Copyright © 2009 by Jenny Blackford

ISBN-13 978-0-9819243-1-1

Published by
Hadley Rille Books
PO Box 25466
Overland Park, KS 66225
USA
www.hadleyrillebooks.com
contact@hadleyrillebooks.com
Attention: Eric T. Reynolds, Publisher

Cover illustration copyright © Rachael Mayo

To Russell Blackford,
who has always said that I should go back
and finish that Classics Ph.D.

Acknowledgments

Many thanks to Russell Blackford, my husband, for his support, encouragement and proof-reading, and to Terry Ryan, my erstwhile Classics lecturer from the University of Newcastle, who generously checked the manuscript for historical accuracy and more. All remaining errors are, of course, my own. Thanks also to Eric T. Reynolds, for publishing my "Python" story and asking me to write more about ancient Greece.

Chapter One—Thrasulla, The Priestess

Delphi, around 491BC

THE SPARTAN KING, KLEOMENES, had the eyes of a rabid wolf. He was half-mad with cunning.

Perialla could not see it, though it was clear to me as daylight. Even now, I cannot understand why Delphic Apollo so blinded his senior Pythia to the madness of the man who wished to use her.

The meeting that day, in the best room of the house that we three priestesses of Apollo shared at Delphi, was Kobon's idea—yet another of his endless self-serving machinations. His father, Aristophantos, was the richest man in Delphi; he swaggered the streets of the town as if the citizens of all Phokis had made him tyrant. At 60, Aristophantos had the look of a proud old bull, master of the herd, and showed no sign of approaching death. It would be decades before plump Kobon inherited his father's wealth; while he waited, he indulged himself in power politics. He glowed with self-satisfaction on the day he brought Kleomenes, king of the Spartans, to meet us in our blue-painted andron—the formal dining room which would have held men's drunken dinner-parties, if Perialla, Diodora and I had not been female, and celibate in Apollo's service.

Kleomenes pretended to pay attention as Kobon droned on about the eternal link of friendship between the peoples of Sparta and Delphi, but one sandaled royal foot was quietly tapping on the floor, betraying the king's impatience. I could only bear to listen to one word in five of Kobon's speech; even that much could have put Prometheus to sleep, despite the agony of the eagle tearing at his liver. The small fire in the hearth of the andron made it cozy, and the carved wooden chairs that the slaves had set in a rough circle were all too comfortable. It would have been far too easy for me to have closed my eyes and fallen into dreams. Instead, I gossiped.

"If Kobon doesn't stop fiddling with that new signet ring," I whispered to Diodora behind my hand, "I'll scream."

"There's no way his wife would have let him *buy* that," she whispered back. "She's pregnant again, and their eldest girl will need a dowry soon. The slaves tell me her periods started last year; her mother won't want to wait too much longer before she gets the girl safely married. She's no great beauty, either."

"Mmm," I said. I'd heard the same things, and come to the same conclusion.

"That ring looks expensive," Diodora said. "The amethyst's a good deep color, and the Gorgon on it was carved by a master." Her fingers traced snake-symbols on her arm. "The workmanship is worth far more than the gold or the stone. I think Kleomenes has been generous to his friend Kobon."

If the prophecies Apollo gives through us are to be useful to those who seek them, we Pythiai need more than ordinary common sense. Good oracles are skilled judges of men and women, and of the little signs that give away their secret desires. When Apollo chooses us to serve him, we must be past the age of caring for men, or of men lusting for us. Fifty years in the world can teach an active mind more than it is comfortable to know of human nature.

"Generous *again*," I said. The gold chain that Kobon had mysteriously acquired last time Kleomenes visited Delphi still gleamed bright around his neck. As Kobon maundered on, he touched the new ring with a fleshy finger, and fingered the blue glass amulet that hung from the gold chain. He gazed at the Spartan king as a lapdog looks at its master. He did not see the madness in those flashing eyes.

My father killed a rabid wolf one winter, back when I was just an ordinary girl of twelve or so, gawky and thin—long years before I was taken by oracular Apollo to be a Pythia. Our dogs were barking as if the sky had fallen, and the sheep were baa-ing loud enough to make it fall. Father and I both went out to the snow-covered farmyard to see what was happening, leaving Mother with my siblings and the slaves indoors, crowded around the warmth of the hearth. The wolf was jumping up against the sheep-pen, snapping at the wood, taking no notice of the noisy dogs. Thick saliva dripped from its jaws. The winter sun was low over the gray-green waters of the Gulf of Corinth far below our stony farm, and the cliffs of Parnassos loomed above us; the wolf's mad eyes seemed bright as torches in the weak late-afternoon light.

Father called back our thin brown mongrel dogs. They slunk to him and cowered behind his legs. They knew the wolf was strangely dangerous; like me, they had a gift for reading the movements of the body. I stood beside my father, deliciously afraid, and glad to be away for once from the women and the endless weaving and spinning. A proper Hellene girl would have been terrified, I'm sure; my mother would have fainted with terror even to know a wolf was near. I, instead, was fascinated by the strangeness of the wolf, the panic of the sheep.

"That wolf's mad, Thrasulla," Father said, holding out an arm to keep me safe behind him. "We mustn't go too near. Fetch me the bow and a handful of arrows, will you? I'll keep my eyes on the wolf. Go as fast as you can. Oh, and take the dogs with you, and lock them inside the house to keep them out of trouble."

I ran to the house with the dogs at my heels, found the bow that always hung near the front door, took arrows from the goatskin bag nearby. I closed the heavy door on the dogs behind me; Mother mightn't like them being in the courtyard by day, but Father could explain later.

Out at the sheep-pen, the wolf slavered and growled. Without a word, Father took the bow and one of the arrows from me and put an arrow neatly through the beast's hairy throat. It didn't seem to notice; it kept jumping up the sides of the pen, frantic to reach the scared, silly sheep that milled pointlessly in circles. I handed Father another arrow, which he shot into its heart, then another. By the time my hands were empty, the wolf lay still on the snow, bleeding from wounds all over its throat and chest. I stood and looked, almost entranced. How strange to see the madness end in bloody death—far stranger than the neat, domestic deaths of ducks and geese destined for the cooking pot.

"If he'd bitten the dogs, Thrasulla, they'd have been mad like him in a month or two," Father said. He took the wolf's corpse by its shaggy tail and started to drag it away from the sheep-pen.

"Or like Glaukos, Nikes' son?" I asked. I was fairly sure, but I wanted to check with the only person whose opinion I really trusted.

Father turned, and looked hard at me. "Tell me about it, daughter," he said.

"It was while you were on campaign with the army last summer. Glaukos was bitten by a mad dog, and his father killed it, but too late. Mother went to try to help the family to heal him, but there was nothing she could do. Glaukos screamed nonsense day after day, and frothed at the mouth. They say he even hit out at his mother and the slaves, before he died. And he would drink nothing for days, though he must have been thirsty."

Father looked at me, his face serious. "You're right. It is the same madness."

"I thought so."

Father's frown deepened. "You see more than other children, Thrasulla. It's not normal."

I shrugged. I'd never been normal. Mother had made that clear from the moment I first spoke—perhaps even before then, but I don't remember that. All of the slaves were afraid of me. Ten or twenty times a day I caught them from the edges of my vision making the sign against the evil eye at me. I didn't care.

I asked, "So if that wolf had bitten me, I'd have been like Glaukos?"

"Yes," Father said, still dragging the wolf by the tail behind him. "Stay away from any sign of madness, daughter."

His tone of voice was odd. I could tell that he meant more than he said, but I was too young to untangle the strands of meaning—to understand what he was afraid to say to me. I just nodded. I would think about it at night, while the rest of the family snored. Sleep had never come easily to me, and tonight would be more difficult than usual, I knew, after the excitement.

Father left the dead wolf on a bare patch of ground far from the sheep or the dogs. He said, "We must purify the carcass with fire."

We walked back towards the farmhouse, to the winter wood-pile. My father placed a load of kindling in my outstretched arms, and took an armful of heavier pieces of wood for himself.

We stood together in silence, wrapped in our thick woolen cloaks—not elegantly, like Mother, but tightly against the snow-cold wind—and watched the fire burn until the wolf was nothing but ashes and gray lumps of bone. Father's red-brown hair glowed in the fire's light.

Chapter Two—Harmonia, The Slave

Athens, Summer, 430BC

THERE SHOULD HAVE BEEN nothing in Aristogeiton's stomach except the water that I had trickled between the boy's bleeding lips over the previous hour, but all the same he retched and groaned until the bowl I held was half-full of foul liquid. The smell in the boy's bedroom was appalling, but a slave must cope each day with things that an Athenian citizen would never endure; I'd had twenty-two years of it, since I'd been born a slave.

"I think that's all for now, Harmonia," the boy said, his voice wavering. "By all the gods, I hope so. That was horrible."

I wiped the boy's raw, bloody mouth with a clean, damp cloth and settled him back onto his pillows.

"Would you like more water?" I asked. For days, Aristogeiton had swallowed all the liquid anyone could dribble into his mouth, but he was still thirsty.

"Soon," he said, too quietly for my liking. "My mouth feels as if it's on fire. But wait a little while, first, Harmonia. I'm so tired."

I carried the bowl to the door. Soon I would go and empty it into the cesspit in the courtyard—but not until he was asleep. Under the vomit in the bowl lurked Medusa's face, painted in red, her tongue lolling from a too-wide mouth, snakes writhing in her hair. The painter had put the angry gorgon in the center of the bowl to avert evil, but the disease that had Aristogeiton in its foul jaws was not afraid of her—or of anything.

16

The boy held up his right hand to me. "Am I dying, Harmonia?" he asked, his voice as brave as an eleven-year-old could make it. He was his father's son and heir; he knew that he was expected to carry on the family name and bear a son to tend the family's graves.

"Of course you're not dying, Aristogeiton," I lied. "In a few years, you will be a strong hoplite soldier just like your father. You will fight the enemies of Athens and win great battles. And you will make wonderful sculptures, just like him."

"I will," he said, half-smiling. "Yes, I will. I'll make friezes for temples, and big, strong herms to stand guard at the front of people's houses, and everything." His swollen eyes closed.

I closed my eyes, too, for a moment. I could not let the boy see me crying. Aristogeiton had always loved the herms in his father's workshop, each with life-like cock and balls protruding from a smooth block of stone, and Hermes' bearded head at the top. But it didn't seem likely that the boy would ever grow up to carve one of them himself. Unless the gods intervened, he would die of this new disease that was sweeping Athens, this plague, and nothing I or anyone else could do would stop it.

I was just one of the family's female slaves, house-born in Athens. I did what I could to help the boy: bathing his head and his hot, reddened eyes; cleaning his ulcerated body; trickling water and thin barley porridge into his bleeding mouth; and stroking olive oil onto his congested, aching chest. It was not enough. Aristogeiton's flesh was cool to the touch, but to him it felt like flames, and all the water in Athens could not cool the fire inside him.

My master Pauson came to the sickroom door. He was not ill like his son, but the lines of his face were harsh in the midday light; they showed how little he had slept lately. He looked at the boy, then looked at me, questioning.

"No change," I mouthed.

He pulled a light chair up to the other side of the bed. "You will get better now, Aristogeiton," he said to his son. "I have given a sacrificial cake to Apollo Far-shooter on our courtyard altar. I promised him that, when you are well again, I will sacrifice a goat to him, and I will carve a statue for his temple from the finest Pentelic marble I can buy. Apollo will help us now. His arrows bring plagues and disease, but he is the Healer as well."

The boy grabbed at his father's hand, and held it tight.

Pauson kept talking, anxiously. Was he trying to convince the boy, or himself? "In a few days it will be the seventh of Hekatombaion, and Athens will celebrate Apollo's yearly feast. The city will sacrifice countless fine cattle to the god, and he will be pleased with all of us. Apollo the Healer will cure you, I'm sure."

"Aristogeiton needs to sleep now, master," I said. Really, it was the master who needed to sleep, and me. Soon enough, unless the healing god intervened, the boy would sleep quietly in his grave forever.

The boy was worst at night, coughing and retching. The night before, he'd thrown up the contents of his stomach four, maybe five times. For the previous seven days and nights, my twin sister and I had nursed him together, dozing on a pallet in the corner when we could. The master had spent the nights in his own bedroom with his wife, as was fitting, but he looked as if he hadn't slept any more than we had.

At least Pauson wasn't managing the sculpture workshop at the same time. With the Spartan army camped in the countryside less than a day's march from Athens, just as in the previous summer, looting and burning, there was more demand for swords and shields than for the works of stone and marble that Pauson usually produced, and the war had put a stop to Perikles' rebuilding of the temples up on the Akropolis. The master's strong male slaves were earning good wages for him in an arms factory owned by his friend Drakes, making bronze weapons for Athenian citizens going off to war.

"I will sit with my son for a while," Pauson said, still holding Aristogeiton's hand. "Go rest, Harmonia, and leave me alone with him."

Before I'd reached the door, Aristogeiton had a fit of coughing, and I ran back to his side. The boy's breath was strangely fetid, like nothing I had smelled before. I took the cloth from his forehead, rinsed it in the jar of clean water at my feet, and wiped his face with it. I rinsed the cloth again, then lay it back on his flushed forehead to keep him cool.

Pauson gave me an exhausted half-smile, and pointed at the door. "Go," he said. "Rest."

How could I rest? I was too worried—about my sister, even more than about Aristogeiton—and my mistress needed to know how her son was now. I nodded obediently to my master, but I carried the bowl of vomit to the cesspit in the corner of the courtyard and tipped it out, then drew fresh water up from the deep well, to rinse it thoroughly.

My mistress Ismenia had most of the women of the house gathered around her in the courtyard, working, as if it was a normal day. The mid-summer sun was high in the sky, now, and the shady side of the courtyard, under the colonnade, was far cooler than the workroom upstairs where we spent most of our days. She'd set up the tall loom in the shade next to the kitchen wall, and was walking back and forth in front of it, pushing the shuttle with the thread through the vertical strands of fine-spun wool. Each pass my mistress made, tall, young Dosis beat the new thread upwards, compacting the weave into good, dense cloth.

Ismenia was still elegant, despite everything. Her long, black hair was carefully piled up into a low bun, and one of the slaves had tied a ribbon around her head; her old-fashioned chiton draped gracefully from two brooches at her shoulders, and the overfold that hung down to her waist was patterned at the edge with fine blue and yellow lines. Unless you looked, you wouldn't notice that her lovely eyes were red from crying, but I'd heard her in the night, when Aristogeiton was quiet.

The mistress' almost-nubile daughter, clever Philinna, sat on a stool nearby, spinning washed and carded wool into fine thread as if it might save her younger brother's life, while a baby girl lay on the ground, trying to catch the spindle whorl in her tiny grasping hands. Expensive toys were scattered all around her: a rattle, a cart with wheels

19

that really turned around, a man riding on a mule—but the spindle whorl moved in the sunlight, entrancing her.

The baby belonged to Pauson's moody sister Kalonike, who'd come to us after the Spartan army had marched over the Isthmus into Attika to ravage and burn the crops and houses of the countryside. Perikles, the strategos who'd led Athens to so many victories, had commanded all those who lived outside the city walls to retreat within their solid protection. Pauson had been happy to take in his difficult sister and her husband, Thaumas, when they'd arrived here, even though he'd said, apologetically, that this house in Athens was small by country standards. Soon, though, refugees from the countryside were camping out anywhere they could, in temples or on any empty land.

Kalonike's grown son wasn't married, and lived with them on their farm, but he'd already been out on campaign when she and Thaumas had come here. Her husband was soon levied to serve as one of the four thousand hoplites whom Perikles took on his triremes to ravage the Spartans' own coastline. It was only Kalonike and her baby here now, in Pauson's house, and the foolish woman mourned her absent men as if they were dead.

The two middle-aged female slaves whom Kalonike had brought to the house with her were busy carding wool, rubbing it on their thighs as they knelt on soft mats on the stones of the courtyard. They spoke to one another quietly in their barbarian tongue from far-off Syria, which I cannot understand. Their city had been captured in a small war, decades ago; the men were put to death, and the women and children enslaved. The two women seemed empty-headed when they spoke to us in the halting Greek that they'd picked up after they were enslaved. For all I knew, though, they could have been talking together about war and politics, or epic verse, or even the strange gods who live in the East, where they came from. Perhaps their lives were deeper and stranger than I ever understood.

Chapter Three—Thrasulla, The Priestess

KING KLEOMENES' EYES, THAT DAY in Delphi, were just like the wolf's back on my family's farm. Ambitious Kobon beside him looked like one of the foolish sheep that the wolf had tried so frantically to reach. Kobon was a powerful and respected citizen of the town most sacred to Apollo Far-shooter, but some god or daimon had blinded him to the danger he was in. Kleomenes had him penned just where he wanted him.

Like any good citizen of Sparta, Kleomenes was clothed more plainly than an Athenian slave. He was one of the Spartans' two kings, and from the senior Agiad lineage, the descendants of the older of the dynasty-founding twins, long resented by the junior Eurypontid line. Nonetheless, the king wore no gold or silver, not even a colored border woven into his rough-spun red cloak. His only adornment was his long, black hair, artfully arranged in ringlets shining with olive oil—but every adult Spartiate was expected to tend his hair in this archaic manner. As far as men could see, he followed every letter of the laws that prophetic Apollo had given from his oracle so long before to Lukourgos—the laws that turned Sparta from a rich state of poets and sculptors to a military compound with no goal but to breed more and yet more citizens to hold the wide lands they'd foolishly conquered. But there was more to Kleomenes than met the casual eye.

Kobon driveled on, giving a long encomium on the fertile plains of Sparta, its admirable educational system, its exemplary hoplites, the benefits of the dual kingship, the undoubted descent of the kings from the hero Herakles, and the many rich offerings that the Spartans had brought to Delphic Apollo over the centuries.

Only a simpleton would try to influence Apollo's priestesses *that* way. Diodora and I signaled our boredom and amusement to one another with subtle movements of our bodies. We were not so easily impressed. We tried to include Perialla in our silent conversation, but she ignored us. That was not so unusual; she was often quiet and difficult, though passionately devoted to Apollo's service. I would speak to her later, I decided, to find out what was on her mind.

Finally Kobon maundered to a close, and it was Kleomenes' turn to try to move us. Even with his wits half-destroyed by madness, this man was far sharper than fat, silly Kobon. We would need to take good care if we were to use him, and not the other way around.

He fixed the three of us with those glittering half-mad eyes, and said, "I will leave the matter of the most appropriate offerings to the god. You, his priestesses, must know what would best please him, whether it is gold for his temple or gold to adorn those who serve him faithfully." He looked hard at each of us in turn, as he said that.

"You Pythiai are chosen from the common people," he said, "not from the aristocrats of Phokis; you have not received rich gifts of gold from fathers or husbands. However, I have consulted with wise men, and as far as they can tell me, there is no rule that says you may not receive such gifts from others—for the glory of your Lord Apollo."

I tried to keep any reaction out of my face, though inside I was snorting with unwomanly laughter at this unsubtle appeal to greed. Perialla, though, gazed straight at the Spartan king, her mouth slightly open, her pink tongue just visible. Diodora gently nudged my forearm with her elbow, apparently innocently; her face was as blank as I hoped mine was. I knew what she was thinking, though not by any arcane means. Such a blatant attempt at bribery! How could Perialla, our senior colleague, possibly be naïve enough to be tempted by it?

"You may have heard some rather indelicate rumors about my fellow king, Demaratos," Kleomenes said, his face a picture of a man talking of scandal while trying not to offend a group of virtuous women. "Well, not so much about him, as about his mother, and his putative father."

I tapped a finger against the curved arm of my delicately carved chair; with its lion's paws for feet and griffins' heads as finials behind my shoulders, it was worth more than the whole contents of my parents' farm. Diodora nodded almost imperceptibly. Indeed, we *had* heard rumors, way back when Demaratos was born. Back then, people said that, when the slave had brought the news to Demaratos' supposed father, the Spartan king Ariston, the king had counted the lunar months on his fingers, and got a number somewhat less than the statutory ten.

Kleomenes said, "Even here in distant Phokis, you might have heard that when King Ariston was told of Demaratos' birth, he said that the child could not be his. You need to know, moreover, that King Ariston spoke these words in front of the incorruptible Ephors of Sparta, elected by our equally incorruptible body of Spartiates. There can be no doubt of what the king said, and when, and why."

I tried to look politely shocked, as a virtuous woman should have been, but every juicy detail was stamped in my mind, as it was in the mind of every woman my age in all of Hellas, and surely as far as the Hyperboreans who live behind the North Wind, out of the arthritis-inducing reach of painful cold and snow. Demaratos' disputed paternity had been the most exciting piece of gossip in the civilized world for several years.

It had been poetic justice, really; the whole thing was King Ariston's own fault. He'd been idiot enough to fall in love with his friend Agetos' beautiful wife, supposedly the loveliest woman in Sparta. Foolish Ariston apparently just couldn't bear to live without her. In his greed and lust, he'd tricked his best friend into divorcing his beloved wife, and giving her to him.

"You know, too," Kleomenes said, "that King Ariston had married twice before, but neither woman had given him a child. One wife might be barren, by the will of the gods, but two in a row? It seems unlikely. The third marriage was a desperate attempt to breed a Eurypontid heir to the double throne of Sparta."

And all of Hellas knew, it was entirely possible that King Ariston's friend Agetos had put Demaratos into his mother's belly well before the Spartan king had married her—which meant that the ruling Eurypontid king of Sparta, Demaratos, was not of royal blood. How could the senior Agiad kings fail to take an interest in this question?

The Agiad king Kleomenes went on chattily, trying to lure us into believing all he said: "Of course, everyone knows that Ariston later declared that the child was his. In his deluded folly, besotted by the charming boy, the longed-for Eurypontid heir at last, he persuaded himself that the child really *was* his—though it was patently impossible. You only have to count the months."

But we three priestesses knew more than that. I am childless, but both Diodora and Perialla had borne strong children before Apollo claimed the women as his mouthpieces. We knew that babies had been born too soon, and lived. Whether Demaratos was one of them, though, we did not know. Only the gods knew, and perhaps the boy's mother.

His eyes glittering, Kleomenes went in for the kill. "Demaratos is the son of Agetos, not of King Ariston. He is not truly of the royal lineage. Leotukhides is the rightful king of the Eurypontid line. Demaratos should be deposed, and Leotukhides raised in his place."

He looked at each of us again, gazing as far as he could into our eyes. People do not normally find looking into the eyes of a Pythia a comfortable business; I doubt that it was easy even for the half-mad king.

He said, "I know what you must be thinking. Certainly, Demaratos is raising calumnies against me at this time, but that has nothing at all to do with the matter of which we speak. It's common knowledge that Aigina betrayed all the other states of Hellas by submitting to Darius, king of Persia, when the foreign king demanded gifts of earth and water. Traitorous Aigina sent the Persian despot the tokens of submission that he wanted."

I nodded. So far, so good. This was indeed known by all with ears to hear.

The king continued: "I went to the craven island, with the full authority of the Spartan Assembly and its Ephors, to arrest the men responsible for this most reprehensible act—but that stupid great ram Krios would not let me take anyone away. He claimed that I'd been bribed by Aigina's neighbor and eternal enemy, Athens." Kleomenes' voice was higher, more excited. He was still furious with this man.

The Spartan king jumped to his feet. "Yes, Athens *had* approached Sparta about Aigina—how could the Athenian people not come to us to aid them against such blatant treachery? We are the only state in Hellas more powerful than them—though they think they are our equals. One day, we will show them our true strength." He looked into the fire, brooding, then spoke again: "But the Athenians did not *bribe* me. It was *Demaratos* who subverted Krios in Aigina, told him to resist my rightful power, put lies into his mouth. The lies are Demaratos' own. Ever since he took power, Demaratos has tried to undermine me."

He stared into the fire again for long moments, lost deep in his resentment for his fellow king. Then, at last, he said, "But it is not *I* who wants Demaratos deposed. *I* do not hate him for his lies. Rather, I fear the anger of Zeus, king and father of the gods, that we Spartans have allowed one to rule us who is not of the kingly line. For the people's sake, he must be removed from the throne."

Chapter Four—Harmonia, The Slave

ISMENIA HADN'T NOTICED ME walk into the courtyard. "Mistress," I said, to let her know I'd come from Aristogeiton's sickroom, so she could question me, if she wanted. "The master is with your son."

She looked at me, too eagerly.

"No change," I said, wishing there were some other news I could have brought.

She wobbled on her feet, as if she might faint. After the last few days, she would be close to the edge of her reserves. But was she pregnant again? Dosis left the loom and took a step towards her, ready to catch her, but the mistress grabbed hold of the back of a chair, and stood tall again.

She said, steadily, as if nothing had happened, "Take some lunch to my husband now, Harmonia. And take some food to Kalonike, as well. Something sweet, something to tempt my sister-in-law to eat."

Her eyes were bleak. We both knew that Kalonike had barely touched food since her husband had marched down to Piraeus to join Perikles' triremes. She was punishing all of us for the danger that Thaumas and her son were in.

My mistress said, "I will not have it said that I let my husband's sister starve, even if she refuses food. Ktema is with her; see if she can persuade her to eat something."

"I will try, mistress," I said. If anyone could persuade Kalonike to do anything, it would be Ktema, the old slave who'd been her nurse when she was a child.

In the kitchen, I found all the delicacies I could gather—cakes made of sesame pounded with the thyme-scented honey of Mount

26

Hymettos, fat purple figs bursting with sticky juices, slices of sweet red watermelon, and chickpeas roasted with cumin and oil, enough for sweet-toothed Kalonike and the old slave who'd nursed both her and Pauson—and put them on a plain, wide earthenware plate.

Next, it was time to put together Pauson's lunch. I found my master's favorite bowl, the one that had been handed down from his father and his father's father. At its center was a portrait of the Pythia, painted in black, seated on the prophetic tripod in Apollo's temple in Delphi. Sadly, no oracle was needed here today to tell Aristogeiton's probable fate. Too many people had died already, here in Athens, of this new plague. Perhaps, though, the boy would rally, and live, as his father still hoped.

Sighing, I put a handful of almonds and walnuts and a few olives into the bowl; that was all the master ever took for lunch. I turned to leave the kitchen, but then I stopped. Today, Pauson needed more. I scooped three pieces of sheep's milk cheese from Sicily out of the brine where they were stored, and put them on top of the olives.

Leaving the bowl I'd prepared for Pauson, I carried the wide plate of delicate foods upstairs to the big room that Pauson had assigned his sister and her husband, and handed it to Ktema at the door. I said, "The mistress asks you, Ktema, please to make sure Kalonike eats some of this today." The old slave nodded. "For Pauson's sake," I added, of my own accord.

For myself, I'd have been pleased if Kalonike had starved herself to death over her fears for her husband and her son, both gone to war. She was too much like her vicious now-dead mother, Damareta, for me to wish her anything but ill. Only a few days earlier, Kalonike had beaten my sister almost senseless, claiming that Eukarpia had done her hair badly, made her look middle-aged; the woman was fast approaching forty, but vain as an adolescent keen to become a bride. The bruises were still purple and green against my sister's pale skin. But while Aristogeiton was so sick, my master didn't need to be distracted by his sister's selfishness; I would do my best to see that she didn't starve.

My duty to Kalonike done, I walked towards the stairs that led down to the dying boy and his father.

* * *

But before I took Pauson his lunch, I went to check on my sister. Eukarpia was curled up on her pallet, snoring, in the tiny room that she and I shared with the other female slaves, Dosis and Ktema; Kalonike's Syrian slaves slept in the room with her, since Thaumas had gone to war.

My sister had been strangely tired while we'd been looking after Aristogeiton overnight, even given that we'd been tending him for seven full days. When the sun had risen and the master was up, before he'd gone off to the agora, I'd asked his permission to send her to bed for the day.

Now I leant over my sister, my beloved twin, Eukarpia. She was so tiny: no larger, it seemed, than Aristogeiton, though at twenty-two years old, we were both twice his age. Her short dark hair, like mine, was lank with fatigue; her skin was oddly flushed. I checked her forehead. It was not hot to the touch, but neither was Aristogeiton's. What would I do if she had this terrible new disease, like him? How could I live without my sister?

I made sure that the blue glass scarab was secure on the leather tie around her neck. The amulet was Egyptian magic, strong against disease, according to the old woman I'd bought it from—but then, she *would* have said that. I kissed it, and prayed to all the gods there were that it might work. Eukarpia made vague, incomprehensible murmurings as I prayed.

Back downstairs, in the sick boy's bedroom, my master was sitting at his son's side, holding one hand. The boy's eyes were closed, but he did not look to me as if he were asleep.

"Why are you not resting?" Pauson asked me, wearily.

"My mistress asked me to bring you some food. Here it is."

I held the Pythia bowl in front of Pauson. He lifted his head a little, and looked at the food as if it were something alien.

"Eat it, please, master. A little of it, at least. Please. You need to eat, for your family's sake." I was gabbling, but I couldn't stop. "You must not get sick."

Pauson looked at me. His eyes were dark, unreadable. He was the gentlest of masters, normally—nothing like his fury of a mother, now dead, thank the gods, or his difficult sister—but his son was dying before his eyes; fear and sorrow could goad people into doing terrible things, and slaves' lives were cheap.

I said, quickly, "Forgive me if I have overstepped my place." I put the plate on the floor, lowered my eyes and bowed to him, as a slave should.

"It's not you that's the problem, Harmonia," he said.

I let out a breath I hadn't realized I was holding, but I didn't say anything. It wouldn't have been proper. I just nodded, mutely, and picked up the plate again, holding it out to him. He *had* to eat, or he would grow weak—and then what would happen to all of us?

Pauson looked at me with those dark eyes, then down at the plate of food, and picked up a walnut. He put it into his mouth, and chewed for what seemed forever.

"I'm sure Perikles is right. This war with Sparta won't last long," Pauson said, but his voice sounded far less certain than his words. "Athens is too strong for them." He chose a piece of salty white cheese. I was glad to see it; if he kept eating, perhaps it would make him strong enough to protect us all through this terrible summer.

"It was our fleet, our strong wooden walls, that beat the Persians at Salamis, back in my grandfather's time," he said. "We had to evacuate our city, and the barbarian Persian army ravaged and burnt it to the ground. They even destroyed the temples of the gods on the Akropolis. But our fleet fought off the most powerful empire in the world." His eyes were pleading with me, or with the gods.

He ate the piece of cheese, then picked up a wrinkled black olive, and looked hard at it, as if it held the key to the war. "This time, we're only fighting the Spartans and their allies, not the Persians. And this time we're staying in Athens, inside the walls, and defending the city with our strong fleet. The Spartan king who leads the troops does not dare attack our walls. Perikles' strategy is good. Athens will survive. Grey-eyed Athena will protect her city."

I said nothing. What does a slave know of strategies of war? I just rinsed and wrung out a clean cloth, and wiped Aristogeiton's ulcerated face with it, as gently as I could. The boy didn't stir; he really was asleep, now, but he looked sicker than ever.

The master ran both of his hands through his hair, then rubbed hard at his tired eyes. "Oh, but it's terrible, Harmonia. Everyone from the whole of Attika is shut up inside the walls of Athens, like pigs in a pen that's just too small. Any farmer knows what happens when you overcrowd your animals, don't give them air, or let them move about. They get sick, and die. Like us."

I looked at Aristogeiton's face in alarm, but he was snoring more convincingly than an eleven-year-old can manage when he's feigning sleep. Pauson slapped his hand over his mouth, but I shook my head. "Fast asleep," I said. It was time the boy slept: he'd been awake all night and morning, and it was past noon, now.

Pauson sighed. "Thank the gods. I'll try to be more careful what I say, in future. Oh, Harmonia, before I forget, I've arranged for a new doctor to come to see my son this afternoon. Maybe this one will have some more helpful advice than the last one. *He* was no use at all. Wait on the will of the gods, indeed. As if we weren't already doing that. As if everyone doesn't do that, every day. Worse than useless."

Ah, I thought, that explained why my sister and I had been given no new instructions, after the doctor had sent us out of the sickroom so that he could examine the boy. Later that day, Pauson had just told us to keep on doing whatever old Ktema had shown us to do.

Pauson said, "You've spent the most time with Aristogeiton while he's been sick, so I want you here to answer the doctor's questions."

I nodded. That was a sensible idea.

"Now," Pauson said, "I really do want you to go and rest. That's a command. I'll send someone to wake you up when the doctor comes." He pointed to the door.

I wrung out the cloth again. I wasn't sure I should leave the boy. He was so sick . . .

"Go," Pauson said. "Rest. I'll sit with my son. Take care of your sister, too. We can't afford to lose her, or you."

Chapter Five—Thrasulla, The Priestess

SINCE I WAS MADE A PYTHIA, I have come to understand what my father meant, when he said, "Stay away from any sign of madness." He feared that my way of looking at the world, the things I saw that others could not see, would drive me mad. But it's not like that at all. People are mad when they cannot see what *is*, when they see instead only what they hope, or fear, or dread. Seeing what *is*, is not dangerous—except when others, whose hopes and fears are stronger than their sense of what is true, distrust the one who sees only what is.

In winter, when Dionysos' nymphs and satyrs romp and frolic on Mount Parnassos, and Apollo leaves his temple, we middle-aged Pythiai of Apollo can go home to the hearths of our disconcerted families. The men and women of my family, on the old farm near Daulis, welcome me each year—but they refuse to accept that I cannot read their minds, and do not know the days of their deaths. Even if I try not to, it's impossible not to read in their eyes and faces the things that they wish to hide: their loves, their hates, their fears, their lusts.

I cannot help but know which of them is having sex with whom, or wants to—or would rather not. Since I was made a Pythia at fifty-one, I've kept my ritual purity, abstaining from sex and certain other pleasures. Even back then, it had been decades since I'd known the touch of a man, but I've still not forgotten the first night with my new husband, almost a stranger at the time, or our first year of marriage.

For the sake of my family's dignity, I pretend not to notice how happy they are when spring comes again and Apollo returns, and they can send me back to the god's sanctuary. If I drape a fold of clothing over my head like a proper, modest widow, they cannot see me smile at the relief their faces radiate as I leave.

After the meeting, when the powerful, foolish men had finally left the house we share, and we Pythiai stood together in the sunny courtyard, Diodora said, "I remember what the Pythia told Kleomenes' ancestor Alkamenes many years ago: 'Eager desire for money will bring the ruin of Sparta.'"

A good try, I thought, but not quite apposite. Hoping I could do better, I said, "But does Kleomenes desire money, or does he merely use it for his secret purposes? Bribery, for example, and corruption. Our informants have told us that he has accumulated far more gold than is sensible for a Spartan, though it is skillfully hidden, but he doesn't seem to use it for his personal pleasure."

Diodora nodded. "You're right. He uses it only to influence others."

Our senior Pythia, Perialla, more than half seduced already by Kleomenes' clever blandishments, was the target of our words. As we ought to have expected, she took no notice of them, but only saw the way we looked at her while we were speaking. Her lips thin and pale, her head drawn up high on her scrawny neck, she said, "You have your mother's anklets of fine electrum, Thrasulla, and gold pins to clasp your chitons at your shoulders. You, Diodora, have rings and chains and earrings almost beyond counting. The slave who dresses you must carry a heavy burden, when you ask her to bring your jewelry box. What do I have? Nothing. One single silver bangle for my wrist. Less than nothing. How can I go into the presence of the god so poorly dressed? He must despise me for my poverty."

In the silence that followed, I could hear the cries of the men and boys of Delphi in the gymnasium a little way down the slope from our house. Their groans and shrieks as they raced and wrestled were like the sounds of distant warfare. I heard the scream of javelins through the air, and the weighty thud of balls of iron as they fell into soft soil.

After a time, Diodora said, "Apollo does not care for gold or other metals. Here in Delphi, the mantic god is interested only in the truth of his oracle." The argument seemed sadly weak to me.

"Oh, really?" Perialla said, her face screwed up with scorn. "In that case, why have the states of Hellas built rich treasure houses in Apollo's sanctuary, all along the Sacred Way that runs from the entrance gate to his beautiful marble temple? Why have they offered the weapons of their enemies as trophies for the god?"

I said, "But that's not—"

Predictably, Perialla ignored my attempt to deflect her from self-destruction. "If, as you say, Apollo does not care for gold or treasure, why then is his temple full of metal tripods, bronze and marble sculptures, and even chryselephantine statues of precious gold and ivory? The fine sculptures on the pediments of the temple, and within the colonnade, the paintings on the walls, does Apollo Far-shooter not care for these rich and lovely offerings? And yet you say the god is happy that I go down into the sacred *adyton* of his temple in un-dyed rough-spun wool without a scrap of gold anywhere about me?"

Diodora said, soothingly, "Mortal men and women care about these things, Perialla. Apollo the Healer is richer than we can imagine. He dwells in Zeus' royal palace on Olympos and feeds on ambrosia. He wants for nothing. He is interested only in your service to him, not in your clothes and jewelry."

"So you say, you with all your anklets and brooches, and your fine-spun chitons."

It was hopeless, but I stubbornly decided to try again. "Diodora is right, Perialla. Apollo is far beyond such concerns. Gold and silver are nothing to him."

"Oh, so that's why people ask him when their ships should set sail, where they should go to found a colony, or whether they should go to war? Rubbish! It all comes down to money, to gold and silver. That's all they want to know about. And he gives them the answers, through us. Then, if the venture brings them money, they reward him with gold; they bring him gifts of gems and finely-worked metal. Why should I not have my share—provided all I say while seated on the tripod is true?"

Perialla's face was flushed, and her mouth was paper-thin with fury. Nothing anyone said could bring her to her senses now. I said, hoping to calm her, "Why should you not, indeed? Provided, of course, that you speak Apollo's words, and not your own."

"I did not say that I would lie," she said. "If all I speak is Apollo's own truth, surely I deserve some small reward, now and then." She sniffed. "In honor of the god, of course."

"Of course," I said, and Diodora echoed it, but I could hear the foreboding in her voice, as she could surely hear it in mine.

We were rescued, temporarily, by our cook, who clattered on the stones of the courtyard to warn us that she was coming, then let us know that dinner would be ready soon. Eunous had doubtless chosen her moment carefully, knowing instinctively from our tones of voice when it was right to intrude; she was a better judge of human nature than any politician. Indeed, she was our best source of news within Delphi, bringing us not only local gossip but also valuable information from all the other city-states of Hellas. Who would be so suspicious that he would guard his tongue around a harmless slave, old and wrinkled, gossiping in the marketplace while she prodded at vegetables and fruit for her owners' next meal?

We took turns in the bathroom, washing before dinner. Perialla went first, snapping loudly at the slaves as usual while they tried to help her. The bathroom was damp when she came out, tossing her head, but two of our slaves poured fresh water from the spring of the nymph Kastalia, heated over the kitchen hearth, into the shallow tub against the wall. Too worried even to enjoy the pleasure of hot water, I barely noticed as the slaves helped me to wash and dry myself. I stood passively as they wrapped my chiton back around my thickening body and led me to my room to do my hair again in the long girlish curls we mouthpieces of Apollo must wear, despite our middle age. I couldn't stop thinking about poor, silly Perialla, and how Kleomenes had dazzled her.

Diodora shook her head ruefully when we passed under the shaded

34

colonnade between the bathroom and our bedrooms, as she went to take third turn to bathe. She was as old as I, but junior to me as a Pythia; she did not prophesy every time mantic Apollo answered men's questions, but remained in reserve, to speak for the god if Perialla and I were both worn out by the god's demands. She looked as worried as I felt about our senior Pythia.

Perialla, I was sure, was blinded by the glint of the gold Kleomenes could give to her, if she would do his will. All she could see was the precious metal that his too-bright eyes half-promised her: jeweled brooches for her simple woolen chitons, rich rings for her wrinkled fingers, worked gold earrings to hang heavy from those sagging lobes. She did not see the madness in his eyes. I did not need to sit on the tripod under Apollo's most holy temple, and breathe the vapors from the sacred cleft in Mount Parnassos, to see that this would not end well.

Chapter Six—Harmonia, The Slave

I PLACED MY PALLET BESIDE my sister's and lay down as quietly as I could, dismayed by the harshness of her breathing.

Despite my care, Eukarpia woke up. "My eyes are sore," she said. "And my head feels like fire." She was almost whimpering with fear.

I felt as if I'd been punched in the stomach. Aristogeiton's sickness had started just like this. No punishment that Pauson's mother had given me, even at her violent, raging worst, had been this bad.

"Show me your eyes," I said, hoping it was nothing. They were as red and swollen as if she'd stood over a smoky fire for hours, stirring a stew. Then she doubled over in pain and coughed, just like Aristogeiton.

How could I live without my twin?

Few slaves ever spend time with their own families. I was so lucky to have had a sister close to me all my life. Our mother was a girl from Thrace, taken from her home and made a slave when she was only nine or ten years old. I'll never know whether the slavers who sold her in Athens had kidnapped her, or bought her from parents who couldn't afford to rear her and give her a dowry; she died before she had a chance to tell me. At any rate, the slavers who put her in chains told her to forget her birth name and called her Thratta, before they sold her.

Pauson's father, old Aristogeiton, bought pretty Thratta as a lady's maid for his fury of a wife. He'd hoped the discontented, aging beauty, Damareta, would be pleased to have a girl to dress her hair and stroke her skin with scented oils. Damareta soon found out that the girl had more skills than that: Thratta's mother had taught her little love spells and household magics before the girl was taken from her home in far-off Thrace. Thratta was *special*. With the girl's potions, Damareta hoped that she could hold her husband's love forever.

But we killed our poor young mother, my twin and I. Damareta punished us every day for that unwitting crime, cursing us to endless torment as she beat us for the least transgression. Even as toddlers, we couldn't understand how it could have been our fault, but we were only slaves, the children of a slave, and our mistress could do whatever she wanted with us.

When we were old enough to understand, and safe in Pauson's house, old Ktema filled us in on how it all had happened. In her greed, Damareta had wondered why she should have only one special Thracian slave, when she could breed another from her. Damareta had waited until the girl was fourteen, as old as most Athenian brides, then she'd chosen Dromon, the handsomest slave in her husband's sculpture workshop, as the father. Damareta had had her eye on him; he was too good to be wasted on mere marble and stone, she'd thought, though she was far too respectable to dally with him herself. But instead of one special baby in Thratta's belly, Dromon had made two, my twin and me: too much.

No one had asked Thratta what she wanted, of course. She was just a slave.

Damareta had unlocked the room the female slaves slept in and sent Dromon to Thratta night after night until the girl's belly swelled. Old Ktema told me that my mother didn't scream and fight, but endured Dromon in silence like a good slave. Perhaps she was even happy that she would be made pregnant; it's a privilege for a slave to be allowed to have a child. She must have been so lonely, a young girl, without her family.

But even one baby might have been too much for our mother, old Ktema told us, and she'd helped deliver babies since she was old enough to understand. Poor Thratta's hands and face had been puffy and swollen throughout the pregnancy—not so unusual, except that a finger pressed into her hand would leave a mark that stayed in her flesh for half a day. Her head had ached continually, too, as she waited for the birth.

Her labor came a month before Ktema had expected it. We were not ready to come out into the world, my sister and I, but we had no choice. As Thratta was screaming with the pangs of labor—happy, Ktema said, that she would soon be a mother—the girl's arms and legs went rigid, and she clenched her teeth so hard she bit her tongue. It started to bleed, but she didn't scream, this time; instead, she convulsed so violently that she flung herself onto the floor.

After that, she fell unconscious, and nobody could rouse her. Ktema pulled my twin and me, tiny as kittens, from Thratta's womb, but she could not revive the dying slave, despite frantic prayers to Artemis, Apollo's virgin twin, protector of women in childbirth. Ktema sent another slave to find the midwife, but it was too late. The woman tried everything she knew, but, in the end, she could only hold our unconscious mother's limp hand until it was time to close her dead eyes, and to leave her shade to wander in Hades.

Damareta had been furious, when she'd heard about the deadly birth. Where would she get her charms and potions now, to hold her husband's love? Who would massage the muscles in her handsome shoulders, drape her dress just so, and pile her hair so artfully behind her head? My sister and I had murdered her favorite slave by being born, and needed to be punished—severely.

If Damareta had simply exposed us both—taken us into the street, left us on a corner or in front of a temple in a kitchen pot as coffin—some passer-by might have taken us in and brought us up as his own slaves. Exposure was too good for us, she'd thought. We needed to feel *real* pain.

Rage made Damareta stupid. She tried to strangle us both, one hand on each of our tiny throats, while the room was still full of women. The midwife gave her poppy juice to drink and soothed her fury, while Ktema took us from Damareta's grasp and carried us to the old master, Pauson's father. The old man, the namesake of his grandson, took us under his protection and gave us our names, and even sent out for a wet-nurse to feed us until we could be weaned onto barley porridge and goat's milk. All his kindness, though, could never stop his furious wife from beating us when he couldn't see her. Eukarpia's right arm was never quite straight again after Damareta broke it in a rage, when she was only three, and the hip she damaged when she pushed me down the stairs still makes me limp when the weather is cold.

When we were six or seven years old, battered and bruised, Aristogeiton's thirty-year-old son Pauson married Ismenia and set up his own workshop. Our master Aristogeiton sent Eukarpia and me off with his son and daughter-in-law, and made over our ownership to him. The old man said that it was so that we could help the young master and his even younger wife, but at that age we would have been more a hindrance than a help.

I'm almost sure the old man just wanted to keep us out of Damareta's vicious reach. He knew his wife well enough to know he could not control her. Damareta died soon after—of fury and frustration, According to Ktema. Eukarpia and I hadn't really believed the news for years; we'd kept expecting her to turn up in the room we slept in, pinching and kicking us. I still have nightmares where she beats my sister, and I cannot stop her.

Sadly, old Aristogeiton did not outlast his raging wife by more than a few months, but I'm sure that he enjoyed the peace without her in his life. As son and heir, Pauson inherited all the old man's slaves, including Ktema. Most of them he sold, but he was still fond of his old nurse, and kept her on. Some of the slaves he sold whispered that the old woman was not worth enough for him to bother selling, but that can't be true; he's fed and clothed her all these years, though she's becoming slow, and he's never beaten her.

Now, on her pallet, Eukarpia coughed and coughed. "My head is so *hot*," she said. "It feels like a ball of flame on my neck. Oh, Harmonia. I've got the plague, haven't I? Like Aristogeiton?"

"Of course not." I tried to put some firm conviction in my voice. She was just tired. She *couldn't* have the plague. My sister could *not* die

39

and leave me here alone. "You're exhausted, that's all. I'm tired, too. We have to rest. Pauson said so."

What happened next made me even more worried. She just said, "Oh, all right," and closed her eyes. In a moment, she was asleep, and her breathing sounded like one of Pauson's men sanding a piece of stone.

I don't know how long I lay beside her stifling my tears, before I slept as well. I would have said I had not slept at all, but I was dreaming of gray-eyed Athena when Dosis woke me. The goddess was shining golden, high up on the Akropolis, beside her glorious new temple, shaking her spear and shield at the Spartan army camped on the plains of Attika. I strained to hear her words . . .

"Sorry, Harmonia, I have to wake you up, the master wants you," Dosis was saying, gently. The tall slave was bending over me, shaking me gently by the shoulder. "The doctor is here."

Eukarpia coughed in her sleep. I put my finger to my lips to make sure that Dosis didn't wake my sister, and crept quietly out of the room, tidying my crumpled tunic and my slave-short dark hair.

Chapter Seven—Thrasulla, The Priestess

CLEAN THOUGH WE PYTHIAI WERE, and scented with the herb-infused oils that the slaves had stroked into our drying skins, our dinner that evening was a miserable affair. We were back in the andron where we'd met with Kleomenes, the ornately-painted room that in any other house would have been reserved for men and their drunken dinner-parties. There was no merriment that evening, though, drunken or otherwise.

The slaves had taken away the chairs the men had used, and brought us tables to eat from. Before we ate, Perialla made the customary small offering to the gods—a splash of wine, a spoonful of the stew, poured out on the small hearth—but after that, she just stared sullenly at the plate her meal was served in, pretending to be fascinated by the Homeric scene painted in red on the burnished black of the wide rim. Now and then she glared conspicuously at my anklets, or Diodora's earrings, but she avoided our eyes like a sulky five-year-old. Diodora and I tried to keep up the pretense of normality, but it would not have fooled even the most unobservant of goat-herds, more used to their strange-eyed flocks than to any human company.

The threat from Persia was worse than ever, Diodora and I loudly agreed. The revolt against the Persians by the Ionian cities had failed utterly, and the Persian victories in Ionia were only going to encourage the foreigners to invade the mainland of Hellas. The great Persian general Mardonius had already taken Thrace and Macedonia into the Persian Empire. King Darius' demand for earth and water from each of the states of Hellas, which Aigina had agreed to, was a pointer to a terrible future for Hellas. The huge armies that the Persian king could

41

command were virtually invincible.

The political situation in Athens looked bad, too, we agreed; the rich and the poor were again at one another's throats—though that was nothing new. Volatile Miltiades, once a tyrant of Thracian cities and a vassal of King Darius, was back in Athens wanting to lead the fight against the Persians, and the unpredictable Alkmaionids might do almost anything. On the other hand, the pottery from Athens' workshops was becoming more beautiful every year. The bowls we were using, gifts from a rich Athenian metic to Apollo's servants here in Delphi, were almost too good to eat from; the gods and heroes painted on them looked as if they could have walked and talked, if they'd chosen to. And if the Persians conquered even feisty Athens, what then?

But something worried me about Athens' fate. If, by the will of the gods, their state escaped destruction by the Persians, what then? In decades to come, would they be so foolish as to pit themselves against their rivals in power and influence, the Spartans? It was all too likely—and they were bound to lose against such well-disciplined hoplites.

Diodora and I moved on to the factional conflicts in Corinth, then looked at one another so glumly I almost had to laugh.

"Well, anyway, Eunous has outdone herself tonight," I said, and took another mouthful of the kid stew. Eunous had braised chunks of baby goat, beloved of Apollo, with onions, garlic, cumin, celery and thyme. Was there some marjoram in there as well, and fresh deep-green bay laurel leaves? Even the barley bread was far more delicious than any I'd ever managed to bake when I was a farmer's wife in Daulis, no matter how much help I'd had from my slaves.

Ever since Apollo established his cult center in Delphi more generations ago than man can count, there's been no shortage here of the luscious flesh of animals—even though the stony slopes of Mount Parnassos could never support more than a few skinny mountain sheep or goats. The divine Healer has ensured that the people of his most precious town do not lack for anything. Homer immortalized the god's cunning in the age-old Hymn to Apollo. The poet tells us that, when the god, in the form of a dolphin, led his future servants here from

Crete, they wondered how they could survive in rocky Delphi, but Apollo said, "Each of you should carry a knife in your right hand and slaughter sheep continually; for they will be there in abundance."

Now, every sacrificial victim brought here from all the city-states of Hellas is fair game for the knives of the citizens of Delphi. There is a proverb: "When you sacrifice at Delphi, you will have to buy extra meat for yourself to eat." The citizens of Athens might laugh about it, in their fine theatre of Dionysos under the stony outcrop of the Akropolis, but it is we who live in Delphi who eat their proud oxen, their tender sheep, and their delicious goats.

That night, Perialla went to her own room after dinner, without a word. After that, she emerged from it only briefly and reluctantly, when she could not avoid it. At first, she would speak of trivia to us if we met around the house, as if nothing was wrong, though her face was white and strained. I made the mistake, one time, of attempting some subtle persuasion while I worked on my embroidery and she sat beside me. After that, she set her face away from both of us, pretended that we were not there at all. Her rudeness to the slaves had always been a problem, but almost every day, now, she beat the girls who washed and dressed her.

Over the years, I'd seen sulks like this when too many unmarried girls were shut up in the house together over winter, with too little to do—but Perialla was a woman well past her child-bearing years, even if Delphic tradition forced us to dress like teenage virgins.

The story was that the Pythiai had once indeed been virgin girls, until some idiot brute from Thessaly abducted and raped a lovely prophetess. After that, women like us, of fifty years or so, were dressed as blushing girls—as if that would fool either men or gods. The tale seemed like one of those answers that men invent when they do not really understand the question. But the gods are not like us, and their ways are unknowable; why should Apollo not have decreed that women long past the age of child-bearing should dress as tender maidens for him?

Through all Perialla's tedious sulks, Diodora and I tried to stay cheerful. Both of us had lived through worse crises, in our five decades on the Earth. My only child had died stillborn, after I'd labored with her for three days. I bled so much that the midwife said another child brought to term would kill me. Diodora's twin sons had lived to manhood, but one died in battle, and the other of his wounds, within a month. Our husbands, too, had died, not pleasantly, long before they grew old; mine of a phthisis of the lungs, hers of a dagger in the chest, a foolish accident in a drunken brawl. Sorrows like these are sent by the gods to all of us, and it is our mortal lot to endure them as well as we can.

Time passed so slowly in our angst-ridden house that it felt like wading through honey, but inevitably the day came around when it was our duty to take turns sitting on the tripod under the temple, and prophesying for Apollo. In the darkness before dawn, we prepared in silence, washing in Kastalia's purifying water, fetched by our slaves from her spring, and dressing up as girls. Perialla's face was pale with resentment, and hard as stone. The blue ribbons in her hair might as well have been laced through the snakes of a stone Medusa's head.

Our senior Pythia looked everywhere except at Diodora and me, but our eyes were drawn against our will to her new jewelry. The earrings were of fine filigree work, with many tiny granulated beads of gold patterning the surface. The bracelets, one high on each of Perialla's arms, were gold snakes, their nuggety heads almost nudging her shoulders under her fine new yellow cloak. I have no fear of snakes—they have their place on Earth, just as men and women do— but these fine serpents made my belly roil with fear. The Spartan king had bought the Pythia with gold. Would she go through with her side of the corrupt bargain?

At last, accompanied by priests and Delphic officials, we set out on foot for the temple above us. The Gulf of Corinth was misty below us, and the rising sun was hidden behind the heights of the Phaidriades— the Shining Ones—the pale stony cliffs of Mount Parnassos that meet in the gorge of the nymph Kastalia's spring, but the dawn light had overcome even the brightest stars. We priestesses walked in solemn procession along the winding path through Apollo's sanctuary, up to his gleaming temple. The milk-white marble glowed in the pale morning light, and the red and blue and gold of the painted areas shone brightly. This particular morning, though, the splendor of the temple made me wince.

Those lovely but expensive marble facings of the temple that I so admired had been a gift to the god from the aristocratic Alkmaionids of Athens, who at that time had been driven into exile from their faction-filled state by the Peisistratid tyrants. The wealthy Alkmaionid family had contracted to face Apollo's temple with ordinary stone, as one of the last stages in its rebuilding after Poseidon Earth-shaker had tumbled it to the ground many years before I was born.

To please Apollo, and perhaps also to please the powerful priests and priestesses of Delphi, the Alkmaionids had used expensive marble facings instead of plain stone. Some say that the family was being pious beyond necessity. Others suspect that their generous "gift" was the reason why the Pythiai of the time instructed the Spartans again and again to drive the tyrants out of Athens, and allow the Alkmaionids back in. Was the fine marble just another bribe?

Apparently, it worked. No matter what the Spartans asked Apollo, back then, every answer the Pythia gave them included the message "First, free Athens." Strangely enough, it was Kleomenes himself, the Spartan king, who took that oracular advice and expelled the tyrant Hippias, Peisistratos' son, from Athens.

That was two decades ago, now, or more. The priestesses involved are dead, walking in Hades' silent kingdom, and I will never know the truth—but as I looked at the beautiful temple, the story of how it came to be so very lovely made me feel uncomfortable. How could Apollo's chosen mouthpiece, a Pythia seated on the sacred tripod, possibly tell lies for gain?

As I walked, I breathed deeply to calm my heartbeat. It would not help matters in the least if I made myself ill with worry. Instead, I attended closely to my immediate surroundings: the broad, smooth stones of the sacred pathway I walked upon, and the fine offerings to Apollo that were set up along the way, given in thanks for the god's assistance in mortal affairs: in business, wars or sickness.

We had already passed the treasure houses of the Sicyonians and many others; now the treasury of the people of Siphnos was on my left, lavishly covered in sculptures of men and gods painted in bright reds and blues and greens. On the pediment towards the rising sun, stone sculptures showed my master Apollo struggling to take back the prophetic tripod which mighty-thighed Herakles had stolen. It calmed me a little; Apollo had been victorious over Herakles in that fight. Herakles was the darling of Hellas, despite Hera's implacable hatred; he'd fought with innumerable opponents and almost always won. You couldn't walk twenty paces here without seeing a painting or a sculpture of Herakles the hero, draped in the skin of the Nemean lion. But golden Apollo had won that particular fight, had seized the tripod back from Herakles and regained possession of his shrine. Surely the god would take care to keep his prophecies pure and untainted this worrying day.

We paced on slowly, passing more and yet more of the gifts that men had presented to Apollo. Indeed, half the states of Hellas had erected fine treasure houses near Apollo's temple, which they delighted in filling with conspicuously glorious gifts to the god. Their piety was often tinged with adolescent boastfulness, but the gifts were lovely all the same, and surely Apollo Far-shooter delighted in them. There were freestanding offerings as well along the path, tripod cauldrons and statues of bronze, or even of gold, but best of all I loved the massive marble sphinx which the people of Naxos gave to the god back in my grandmother's time, setting it up high on a tall marble pillar below Apollo's temple. The sphinx's enigmatic smile hung on the air, reminding me of so many of the ambiguous god's less transparent prophecies. If only Perialla could follow her example!

Even now, in the clear, cool air of dawn, none of the men in the sacred precinct cared to look upon the glorious treasure houses, the smiling sphinx, or even the offerings of precious metals. Already, by the great altar in front of the temple, would-be petitioners impatient for answers stood in a rowdy rabble. Each clutched, as if they might save his life, at the fine beast that he had brought for the god, and at the sacrificial cake sold at huge profit by the priests of Delphi, a heavy tax on anyone seeking answers from Apollo. Perhaps, if the question was important enough, the answer would indeed save someone's life. The anxious crowd seethed like ants on the corpse of a beetle.

Even when Apollo spent his time with us at Delphi, and had not relinquished his place to Dionysos for the winter, he spoke through us, his Pythiai, only for one day a month: on his birthday, the seventh day after the new moon. Too many people had too many questions for Apollo. The priests could only manage the crush by allocating places in the queue by lottery.

The men with questions for the god moved from foot to foot, peering into the temple or up at the sky, restlessly, each of them hoping that the lottery would fall on him first. It had long been rumored, though, that a hefty enough gift to Apollo placed into the hands of his priests—nothing as indelicate as a *bribe*—could miraculously gain the giver an early slot in the long day.

As we passed the great altar standing in front of the temple, I touched my hands to my lips in greetings to the huge bronze wolf set up beside it, a votive gift to Apollo Lukeios from the people of Delphi themselves. Some wise men say that Apollo Lukeios is the god of light, but most Hellenes know him as a wolf, a *lukos*. Sitting on the tripod under Apollo's temple, I have felt the god within me, ravening and merciless, month after month. I am sure beyond all doubt what his holy epithet really means. He is a wolf.

The details of the shining marble columns at the front of Apollo's temple were picked out in blue and gold. On their front face, wise words were inscribed: *meden agan*, "nothing in excess," and *gnothi seauton*, "know yourself." I shook my head. If only it were so easy! Life here in Hellas would change utterly. Who really knew herself, or himself? I knew I didn't—which was far more than most people knew.

47

We three Pythiai slowly climbed the brightly painted marble steps, and stood together between those columns of wise counsel in the porch of the temple, watching as the preliminary sacrifice was carried out, the act that would tell us whether we would speak for the god that day. I could feel Diodora's strain as she tried not to look at Perialla's new bracelets and earrings, gleaming in the growing light. The senior Pythia moved her head and arms this way and that, swaying and nodding, making the gold catch the light, smiling like a child with her first cane hoop to play with. The baubles were lovely; the Spartan king had excellent taste. But what would those finely-wrought earrings and bracelets cost her, in the end? Worry moved in my bowels like a poisonous snake.

As usual, the priests and attendants poured libations of wine and cold water over the garlanded goat; and as you would expect, in the cold morning air, it shivered and shook all over as it was meant to do. The priests were content; Apollo was ready to prophesy. It made me want to laugh, each time it happened: if someone had poured cold water over my head, as I stood on the porch, I would have shivered too, right down to my toes. There are stories, it is true, of times when the beast has stood impassive and unmoving even when drenched with water, and everyone has been sent away. Goats can be strange and stubborn animals—and so can human beings.

Chapter Eight—Harmonia, The Slave

THERE WAS NO SIGN OF ISMENIA, as I walked down the stairs and along the colonnade to the boy's sickroom, nor of her sister-in-law, or either of their daughters. All of them were doubtless safely hidden away from the doctor and his staff, in the women's workroom—like the virtuous citizen women they were, too precious to be seen by strange male eyes. A slave like me was different: my virtue was not so delicate as to need such shielding from an onlooker. Indeed, if Pauson wished it, he could still sell my body to the highest bidder, whether just for the evening or for the rest of my life, even though I've long passed the age where an Athenian citizen's virgin daughter is married off to the son of one of his friends.

I stood outside Aristogeiton's room, worried at what I'd find within, and worried about my sister. I took a deep breath, and pushed the door open.

The doctor here today was fatter than the one who'd visited three days before, and dressed far more expensively, but he looked even more tired, if that were possible. His handsome slave was yawning as he stood with a jar in one hand: Aristogeiton's urine, to judge by the smell, and by the young master's embarrassed look.

Pauson appeared relieved when he saw me. He said, "Here's one of the slaves who's been looking after my son."

The doctor squinted at me, then waved a plump arm dismissively. He spoke to Pauson, not to me: "We don't need her here. There's no doubt about the diagnosis. Send her away." He was not an Athenian, to judge by his accent. He sounded as if he came from one of the islands of

Ionia, part of Athens' wide empire.

I was born here in Athens, and my accent is pure Attic; any non-Athenians, even the people from my mother's country, Thrace, sound uncouth to me. However quaint the doctor's accent, though, the islands have a reputation for learning that all Athenians respect, even slaves.

When the doctor dismissed me, his slave screwed up his face in semi-comic sympathy, behind his master's back. He was tall and well-made; I'd have winked at him in thanks, except that I was so worried for my sister, and Aristogeiton. The sick boy looked so small and terrified, there in his bed, and I could almost *feel* Eukarpia's sickness even though we were many paces apart from one another.

Pauson said, "Stay with us, Harmonia." He looked at the doctor oddly, then, and said, "Let's all leave the boy to rest, shall we, while we talk?"

He led the doctor and the slave out of the door. I paused to send a reassuring smile and a wave to poor Aristogeiton, then followed the men along the colonnade outside it. Pauson took them as far from Aristogeiton's room as they could walk while staying within the house. By the time I caught up with them, the doctor had already started to hold forth.

"—his urine, his stools and his phlegm," he was saying, "I can have no doubt at all that what the boy is suffering from is the new plague that is attacking half of Athens. I trained in the temple of the healer Asklepios, son of Apollo, on the island of Kos. I can set a broken arm or leg so that you would never know it has been hurt, and I can treat the sacred disease, but even my master, the divine Asklepios, could not cure the boy of this illness."

I felt as if I had been punched in the stomach. *What if my sister has it too?* Pauson raised his arms in the air and opened his mouth, but before he could speak, the doctor went on: "I am not saying that the boy will necessarily die. Not all who have contracted the disease have died; and of those who lived, none yet has contracted it again. But—"

Pauson put his hands up again, wanting to interrupt, but the doctor took no notice. As if lecturing a group of mildly interested men, rather than counseling the father of a dying son, he said in ringing tones, "Those few who live are often maimed—blind, or lame, or worse. Eventually, the disease attacks the fingers and toes, the eyes, even the genitals. Some lose their memory, for a time or permanently." His slave, behind him, winced and looked away.

Pauson grabbed at a column for support. His face was pale as milk. I must have looked the same, if anyone had looked at me. Perhaps the handsome slave did, then, but all I could pay attention to was the pompous doctor, and his terrible words.

The doctor glanced at Pauson, but just went on speaking. If I'd not been a mere slave, a powerless chattel, I'd have been tempted to kick the brute for his lack of sense. "The air of Athens is filled with a miasma," he said. "It is corrupt with the seeds of this new disease. Doctors from the temple where I studied say that they saw something like it in Lemnos, some time ago, but nowhere near as severe as this, or as deadly. They say that this deadly plague has traveled to us in Athens from far-off Ethiopia, close to the sun. It ravaged Egypt and Libya, next. It was diagnosed down at the port, in Piraeus, soon after the Spartans arrived in Attika."

Pauson, his voice steady but his face still white, said, "Some say in the agora that the Spartans poisoned the reservoirs near the port. They say that none of the Spartans has fallen ill."

The doctor waved his pink hand dismissively, from the direction of Piraeus down by the sea to the Akropolis shining above us in the brilliant afternoon sunlight. "This disease does not stem from a simple poison, with a simple antidote. It is not so easy. There was no poison. The reason why the Spartan soldiers have not fallen ill is simply that they are not living in the same polluted miasma that we are here in Athens, not breathing the same corrupted air."

Pauson sagged a little further, as I suspect did I. One more small hope was lost to both of us. But perhaps Eukarpia was only tired—or maybe it was just a summer cold, in all this unhealthy heat.

The doctor, paying little heed to Pauson, and even less to me, said,

"Now, as to what you can expect with the boy, listen carefully. The disease proceeds from the head, through the stomach, to the bowels. It has attacked his head already; you have seen his ulcerated tongue. Currently, it attacks his chest and stomach; the boy coughs and vomits, expelling from his body all the humors known to medical science. His fever will come to a crisis in the next day or two. Keep him cool, and keep him clean. Use plenty of clean, cool water for the ulcerations on his skin. Poppy juice may help, a little, with the pain, if you can get it. I have none left in my dispensary. That's all that you can do."

The slave closed his eyes and looked away again. It was good to see that he was not oblivious to the pain the doctor was causing, so unthinkingly. How did he cope, working with the doctor, hearing such things from his owner day after day?

"That's all?" Pauson echoed the doctor's words.

"The boy will probably succumb to the fever over the next two days. If he doesn't, then the disease will attack his bowels, and diarrhea will follow. That phase will be painful and protracted, and he will almost certainly be weakened so badly that it will kill him. And remember, if by the will of the gods he survives, he could be maimed, or blinded."

Pauson looked close to fainting. My own stomach felt so hollow that I wanted to throw up. Poor Aristogeiton. Poor Eukarpia. But maybe...

"And now, about my fee," the doctor said. The slave, behind him, shook his head. I don't know if he understood the look of sympathy I gave him then.

Chapter Nine—Thrasulla, The Priestess

THE PRIESTS OF APOLLO LED US from the porch of the temple and through the *naos*, its great central room, open only to Apollo's servants and those strangers who had performed the required rituals. The *naos* was stuffed so full of precious offerings to the god that we could hardly thread our way through the crowded thicket of votive tripods and brilliantly decorated statuary. Servants were sweeping the limestone floor with brooms made of fresh branches of the bay tree, sacred to the god, or washing it with water from Kastalia's spring; and local women were tending the eternal fire on Apollo's hearth, feeding it slowly with pine, his chosen wood, making sure it would never go out.

We greeted the women decorously—Apollo knew, the priests would never recover from the shock if ever they learned how we women spoke when we were alone together—as we threw fresh bay leaves and barley groats onto the eternal fire, to purify our bodies for the god's service. The sacred smoke billowed up around us, and we breathed in the fumes. The smoke would cleanse us inside as well as outside, prepare us for the inspiration of the god. Our bodies were already well-washed in Kastalia's purifying water, but servants of the god sprinkled us now with yet more cleansing drops from the same sparkling spring.

Next to the inner hearth was the *adyton*, Apollo's most secret and sacred place, which few but we, his priestesses, might enter. Hardly more than a small roofed room a flight of narrow steps down from the spacious temple's marble floor, it was as crowded as the rest of the temple with sacred and precious things. An image of Apollo in marble, skillfully-painted in blue and green and gold, took pride of place; the god's long hair hung in shining ringlets down his slender back. The omphalos, the navel of the Earth, stood there near it, a rounded cone of stone draped in sacred ribbons of new wool. It was flanked by statues of the eagles that Zeus once sent from east and west to find the center of the Earth. They met right here in Delphi; this is how we knew that we lived in the very center of the Earth. A bay laurel tree, beloved by Apollo, grew there too, next to the grave of Semele's son Dionysos, god of wine and ecstasy.

Some are surprised that Dionysos has a grave here in Delphi, when he walks alive upon Parnassos every winter with his ravening satyrs and his raving women. But even father Zeus has a birthplace on his holy island of Crete—the cave on Mount Ida, where the Kouretes clashed their swords on their shields to protect him from his father Kronos. There is a grave of Zeus, too, on the island, which the locals will show to interested visitors, for a small fee. The Cretan people are proud of their connection with the king of the gods, just as the locals here are proud to serve Apollo, and prosper in the process. Too many curious travelers to ignore have returned from fertile Crete with tales of visiting the holy places where Zeus was born, and died. Indeed, trustworthy men say there is a grave of sensuous Aphrodite on her island of Kypros, and who can deny her power over us? It seems that she, like savage Dionysos and father Zeus, has died and been buried, but what is death, or life, to the gods? They are above such things, as we are above the worms that live in the soil.

Most important of all the treasures in the *adyton* was the bronze tripod that stood over the cleft in the side of Mount Parnassos. That was where, each in our turn, we three Pythiai would sit, breathing in the sweet vapors that rose from the fissure in the side of the mountain, and listening for the voice of the god. Men had built Apollo's temple here, long ago, to capture the vapors that rose from the rock. That temple fell, destroyed by Earth-shaker Poseidon, and another was built, and another, until the people of Hellas joined together to build the lovely temple where I now stood, consumed with cares.

Some say that before Apollo came here, in the earliest days, there was a shrine of Ge, the Earth, who inspired her priestesses to prophesy. This may be true; she is the mother of us all, and full of knowledge. Some say Apollo killed her wise and holy Python, a monstrous serpent that had slithered through her rock, and took its oracular power for himself. An old woman told me, once, that Apollo put the Python's bones inside the oracular tripod, and that we prophesy through the ancient snake's power. One day, when I am very old, when I fear my time as a Pythia is coming to an end, I will defy the male servants of the god. I will take up the lid on the shallow cauldron set into the bronze tripod, and I will see who or what is buried there.

This was not the time for such a dangerous experiment. Perialla waited with Diodora and me for the first inquirer to be brought through to us by his city's local sponsor, after giving his sacrificial cake and his fine sheep or goat to Apollo. Each of us now held a fresh branch of bay laurel, its subtle smell aromatic even among the altar's smoke. Our heads, already ribboned and garlanded as if we were blushing virgins, were crowned with wreaths of bay leaves, too, ready for the service of the god. Perialla's fine new jewelry shone bright even in the treasure-crowded temple, packed as it was with polished metals and brilliantly-painted stone and wood, and lit with ever-burning fire and endless oil lamps.

Perialla, as the senior Pythia, was always first to descend into the *adyton* to prophesy. Diodora and I looked anywhere but at Perialla's gold, but the fact of what she must have promised was burned into our minds as we waited.

There was a bustle near the hearth, and the first questioners stepped into our view, with their sponsor. Immediately, I recognized the local man whose privilege it was to bring before Apollo anyone from Sparta with a question for the oracle. As I had feared since that ill-omened interview with mad Kleomenes, sacred messengers had come to us from Sparta, seeking an oracle. Of course Kleomenes had made sure, through Kobon, that the Spartan messengers were given the first place in the queue.

The worry that had been writhing inside me like a serpent bit me sharply in my bowels. I pressed my lower lip with my teeth to stop myself from crying out aloud in fear, and clasping my cramping belly.

"Perhaps I should go first today, Perialla," I said, without much hope. "You look a little tired this morning."

She barked a harsh laugh. "Not so fast, Thrasulla. I am senior Pythia. I will descend first into the *adyton*, as is my right."

Perialla signaled to one of the servants of the god who stood around us. "The water, now," she said. The tall young man, dressed in pure white, garlanded with bay, dipped a silver cup into a wide gold bowl filled with sweet water from the spring of Kassotis, and handed it to the Pythia.

Kassotis was a powerful nymph: her water helped to bring Apollo's words to us. Her spring was a little higher up the mountain's side than the temple, but then it ran underground, and emerged again beneath the temple's main marble floor, flowing deep in Apollo's most private *adyton*. A stone channel carried the water beside us while we sat on the tripod and prophesied.

Perialla raised the cup to her lips. She drank the water proudly, looking me straight in the eye.

Chapter Ten—Harmonia, The Slave

I COULDN'T FACE GOING BACK to the room where my sister was sleeping, and disturbing her. She needed to sleep, to get well. She *couldn't* have the plague. It was just a summer cold, I told myself as firmly as I could.

I went along the colonnade to the kitchen, thinking to fill the sick-feeling hollow in my belly with some barley bread, and startled old Ktema sitting on a chair behind the kitchen door.

"Did you hear what the doctor said?" I asked, knowing she must have. Why else would she have been in the kitchen at that time?

She nodded, her wrinkled lips pursed. "Of course. That fancy doctor wasn't exactly tactful with the bad news, was he?"

I sniffed. "Poor Aristogeiton."

"Yes, poor kid. He's too young to die. But living on as a cripple—that would be hard for him. How would he cope?"

She was right. "Losing some toes wouldn't be so bad," I said, "but if he loses the use of his fingers, how could he become a sculptor, like his father?"

Her face screwed up. "What if he loses the use of his cock? That would be worse. All that carousing until dawn that men do, with pretty boys and flute girls—it would all be pointless, for him. Would his life be worth living?"

And how would he produce a male heir? "I suppose he could adopt a child," I said. "Maybe Kalonike's daughter will have a son."

Ktema shrugged, sadly. "It's in the lap of the gods," she said. "Maybe Apollo will answer Pauson's prayers, and heal him."

57

And my sister. It's just a summer cold.

Wisely, Ktema changed the subject. "I'm going to make up a cup of kukeon for the mistress," she said. "I know it's old-fashioned, and the fine city folks here in Athens say it's only fit for peasants, but it will do her good. She's been going downhill every day, since the kid got sick. Now I think on it, a cup of kukeon would do Eukarpia good, as well."

Ktema looked at me then, as if to ask, "Is your sister any better?" She was too tactful to ask out loud.

I gave my head the tiniest shake, not wanting to admit what I feared.

Ktema said, "We can make some extra for her. We'll use thyme to flavor it; the mistress doesn't like the taste of pennyroyal. It's just as good that way. That's what my old mistress used to say, anyway. She was a darling." She smiled.

Had she lost her mind in her old age? "You're not talking about Damareta, are you?" Pauson's evil bitch of a mother had beaten Ktema almost as often as she'd beaten my twin and me, and just as savagely.

Ktema snorted. "Ha! That old sow! Hardly. No, I meant the woman whose family owned me before the master, old Aristogeiton, bought me to nurse Pauson. They had a small farm, out near Eleusis—grape vines, mainly, for wine, and a few olive trees. They were lovely people, much easier to get along with than the beasts who'd owned me earlier—the men who bought me from the slavers, here in Athens."

She made a face, at that, and spat out of the kitchen door into the courtyard.

It wasn't polite to ask too much about another slave's background, but if she was willing to talk, I wanted to hear her story. "You came from Skythia, didn't you?" Her Greek was good—much better than that of slaves taken at fifteen years or older, who never quite get their tongues around the language of their masters—but her Skythian accent was very strong.

Ktema nodded. "I don't know, any more, how old I was. I know my periods hadn't started when they caught me. The raiders swept though our town, captured a dozen girls working in the fields, including me, and were off, before our menfolk even knew they'd been there. Suddenly, I was standing on a block in the slave-market, being auctioned. The men who bought me put me on a ship, and sold me over here."

"But the people who bought you then? They were—"

Ktema made the sign against the evil eye. "The least said about those bastards the better. I still have nightmares. That bitch Damareta was a sweetheart in comparison. Now and then, these men threatened to sell me down the mines in Laurion, when what I did didn't please them, or their customers. I used to wish they would. The mines couldn't have been worse." Her eyes were dark with memory.

"Really?" I'd heard Pauson's friends shouting in delight about the silver mines, and how the coins marked with Athena's owl that the mint struck from the precious metal were the basis of Athens' wealth and power—but slaves were all too aware of the dark side of the mines. We whispered about them in the agora, or in quiet corners. Free men and women avoided the silver mines, if they could; they were too dangerous. No one lived long, working in those deep tunnels; if rockfalls didn't get the miners, the poisonous dust rotted their lungs and their guts. The small army of slaves who processed the ore above ground, washing and smelting it, turning it into good silver to be struck as coins, were not much longer-lived. Being sent to the mines was the worst punishment any master could threaten a slave with, except torture.

If Ktema's early life in Attika was worse than the silver mines, she'd earned every wrinkle in her cheeks and neck, and her gray hair. I'd seen the scars that covered her body, and thought them all inflicted by vicious Damareta. Some of the scars were in places I'd thought strange; I'd assumed Damareta's whip had hit the wrong target, by mistake, and flinched at the thought. Now that I knew why they were there, they made me sad, and angry.

As if she could read my mind, Ktema said, "Oh, they were real bastards, those men, worse than any mine could ever be. I'd have killed myself, if I'd known how. I was too young, and too scared of them, even to try. Anyway, the fools gambled all their money away, and had to sell all their assets, even me. That was when these farmers bought me, the ones I was telling you about, near Eleusis. Best day of my life, it was. I couldn't believe my luck."

She leant over to pat my knee, as if to console me for the bitterness I felt on her behalf. There was nothing I could say, nothing at all, in the face of such courage.

"Anyway," she said, "the mistress on the farm used to make a kukeon whenever the kids were sick, or when her husband had a hangover, which was pretty much every day. Different people make it differently, she said, but she used barley meal, grated cheese and some wine, if her husband hadn't drunk it all."

I mimed lifting a cup to my mouth, and she nodded. "That was their big problem. They grew barely enough food on the farm to feed themselves, and most of the wine he made went straight into his belly, or his friends'. They couldn't afford to keep me on after their kids were old enough to get by without a nurse. They were good people, though. I had plenty to eat, there, and he never beat me, even when he was falling-down drunk." She clicked her tongue on the roof of her mouth. "The baby daughter I nursed there is probably a grandmother by now."

I did a quick calculation. Pauson was well over forty, surely, closer to fifty, perhaps, and Ktema must have been at least twelve years old to have been any use as a nurse to this family she was talking about, years before Pauson's father bought her. She'd be seventy, soon—a fine age for a slave to reach.

"Ah, well," she said, sighing. "For all I know, they could all be dead. More likely than not, I suppose. The gods in their mercy strike down most of us mortals before we get to forty, whether in warfare or in childbed." Painfully, she got to her feet. "Anyway, I'll get a sprig or two of thyme from the plant in the courtyard, for the kukeon. Put a cupful of fine-ground barley flour into a bowl for me, will you?" She walked out of the kitchen.

I found the big amphora of barley flour, and I was bending over it, scooping some into a wide, deep bowl, ready for Ktema to add the wine and the cheese, when I realized that she was back in the kitchen, and was looking hard at me.

"Give that to me, Harmonia," the old slave said. "Sit down over there. You're so pale I can hardly see you against the white of the wall. How long is it since you've eaten? You haven't had dinner with the rest of us for days, since you've been nursing the young master."

I thought about it. It wasn't easy; my head was throbbing as if someone had hit me. When had *that* started? Maybe when I was listening to that insufferable pig of a doctor?

Food, I thought. I'd eaten nothing since dawn; I'd been too busy, and too worried. Then I remembered seeing Ktema kneeling over a brazier in the courtyard in the evening, stirring a shallow bowl of fresh green broad beans, with deep pot of barley meal and water simmering beside her. I said, "I had broad beans and onions last night, with barley mash."

Ktema shook her head. "I don't think so. I fried up some leeks and garlic, last night, to put on the fresh barley bread that Pauson got from the baker, and crumbled some cheese over it. I grilled fat anchovies, as well, for the family. Broad beans and mash were what we all had for dinner the night before. You haven't eaten for days, Harmonia."

"Oh." I said. Suddenly, it was all I could do to keep my throbbing eyes open.

Ktema said, as if to a small child, "You go to bed. I'll take a cup of kukeon to the mistress, then I'll bring some for you and your sister. Go on, stand up, get yourself up the stairs to bed."

And, when I just stood there, helpless to move, "*Go!*"

I was deeply asleep on my pallet, next to my sister, when Ktema woke me with thyme-scented kukeon in a huge two-handled black cup. Athena's owl was roughly painted on the front in red and pale gray. I hoped it augured well for the protection of the goddess on all of us; I'm sure Ktema wished it so.

Ktema sat and watched me drink the kukeon, while I watched Eukarpia drink the one that the old slave had brought for her, in a matching owl-painted cup. It tasted wholesome: thick, medicinal and gluggy, hard to swallow. I could feel it doing me good as I got it down, gluey mouthful after gluey mouthful, under Ktema's approving eye. Eukarpia coughed, but she got it all down in the end.

I don't remember handing the cup back to Ktema, or lying down again. Sometime after sunset, Ktema woke us both to eat a bowl each of lentils and greens, with vinegar and olive oil, and some coarse barley bread to mop it up. They were very plain, but good all the same. Once I picked up my spoon, I couldn't stop eating until the bowl was empty, even though Eukarpia was coughing too much to eat. I coaxed her gently until she'd cleaned the bowl.

"There," Ktema said, taking away the empty bowls. "You two were starving. No wonder you looked so terrible. Now, both of you, go straight back to sleep. I've told the mistress, don't worry. She says you have to rest." She stood at the door and smiled back at us. "It's just like looking after Pauson and Kalonike again. They were sweet kids." She looked as if some memory disturbed her. "Well, *he* was, anyway. She was a little bitch, from the moment she could speak."

After that, I slept again. I must have woken two or three times, but I was too tired to do more than pee in the pot in the corner. The few times I woke, though, Eukarpia was coughing, and her rattling breath troubled my dreams all night. Her mouth and tongue were growing strangely foul, like Aristogeiton's. I said, again and again, aloud and silently, "It's just a summer cold. Don't worry." I dared not look inside her mouth, in case I found ulcers there.

In my dreams, the goddess Athena stood high on her Akropolis, on the roof of her great temple, rattling her spear against her shield.

Chapter Eleven—Thrasulla, The Priestess

THE FACES OF THE SACRED MESSENGERS were blank with Spartan discipline. Accompanied by their smiling local sponsor, the men sat on gilded chairs, waiting for the Pythia to be ready for their question. Several of Apollo's white-clad priests watched over the proceedings. At last Perialla, dripping with gold jewelry, her garlanded head held defiantly high, walked slowly down the steps to the lowest and most sacred part of Apollo's temple, where the sweet-smelling vapors that inspire our prophecy rise from the famous crevice in the rock. I could feel the tension in Diodora's body, as she no doubt felt mine, while we watched Perialla settle herself on the circular cover set into the bowl of the oracular bronze tripod.

Defiantly, almost theatrically, Perialla breathed the sweet vapors that rose around her. She did not look at Diodora or me, but every action or gesture was aimed at us. Her posture and her movements shouted an unmistakable message: no matter what we thought, she would go through with her plans. She saw nothing wrong with what she was about to do.

I couldn't help myself. "It's not too late," I said, quavering like an old woman, but Apollo's servants clustered around me, shushing me with soft noises. Perialla gave no sign that she had heard, although I knew she had.

I stood then quietly with Diodora, watching Perialla's doom unfold. We both knew in the depths of our bellies what her answer would be to the Spartans' inevitable question, even though she would ensure that the priests and other observers could not deny that all had been done correctly. She was prepared to go through all the motions.

And so, Perialla, senior Pythia in Apollo's service, signaled to one of the priests that she was ready to prophesy. One of the Spartans stepped forward, lean-muscled, his red cloak threadbare with age. Steadily, he asked his question: "Is Demaratos the son of Ariston?" His voice was strong and firm; he gave no sign of nervousness. It seemed that he had no idea that what he was doing was such an impious act that any normal man would be in terror of divine punishment.

Perialla held onto the branch of bay laurel in her hand as if it were a queen's scepter. Loudly, she replied, "Demaratos is not the son of Ariston." The sacred messengers from Sparta nodded and walked away, through the treasure-crowded temple, their faces impassive. It was over.

Whether Perialla had told the literal truth or not, she had cheated the god. The prophecy she had given was not inspired by Apollo, but only by her greed. The male priests could not tell, but Diodora and I knew the terrible truth.

Her treachery against her office complete, Perialla left the tripod. "I'm tired, now, Thrasulla," she said. "You can take over." Even speaking directly to me she avoided my eyes, looked at my feet instead. Yet her face glowed with triumph.

Perialla had won the day, or so she must have thought. She sat near Apollo's famous hearth and gazed on us in scorn as the long hours passed and we descended again and again into the *adyton*. The expression on her face said that we were fools to labor so for no reward.

All that terrible day, Diodora and I gave oracles to questioner after questioner, giving the best answer that we could, often surprised by the direction in which Apollo took us. The sweet vapor rose strongly from the crevice in the rock, and the god's inspiration was strong too. Occasionally, deep in the prophetic work, I forgot what Perialla had done, but then I would remember, and wince.

If only some enquirer had come to us and asked, "What will happen to Perialla?" —what would the god have said?

After scarcely more than the handful of days that it would have taken for the messengers and their escorts to march back to Sparta, and others to return, Kobon came to us with the news that King Demaratos had been deposed. The citizens of Sparta had trusted Apollo's oracle, of course, and had stripped Demaratos of his kingship, giving him instead some minor office in their warlike city. Kleomenes' friend and ally Leotukhides had been made king in Demaratos' place. Furious with his countrymen, Demaratos had fled to Elis, then Zakunthos, then finally the east; perhaps the King of Persia would receive him.

Poor silly Kobon beamed as he delivered this terrible news, and rubbed his hands together. Perialla smiled at him as he spoke, her face as condescending as an ancient queen's, and subtly adjusted the expensive-looking folds of her new purple chiton.

"How is your lovely wife, Kobon?" she asked, shaking her head to make her gold earrings tinkle.

My mouth almost dropped open before I could control it. "Lovely wife"? Had I heard right? Times more than I could count, Perialla had called the woman a boring cow, or a foolish over-fertile bitch. Within the privacy of our house, she'd roundly catalogued the faults of all the wealthy wives of Delphi. What daimon had entered into her?

Later that same day, Kobon's wife sent several well-clothed slaves to escort Perialla to her home. The Pythia was to dine there with what the slaves had been told to describe as "a select group of Delphi's most interesting women." Perialla came home looking as smug as the cat that's stolen the cheese from the kitchen, and went straight to her room. After that, she lunched or dined each day with women from the richest families in Delphi, glancing at us with open scorn each time she left the house.

Diodora and I shook our graying heads together. What could they possibly speak of together, the empty-headed women of fashion and the corrupted Pythia in her new finery? Gold jewelry, perhaps? Surely, for her, it would be even worse than sitting in her room, alone, pretending we did not exist?

Our cook Eunous came to us during this time, after her trip to the marketplace for food and gossip, snorting with amused fury. "The word around town," she said, "is that you two are puffed up with pride in your sacred office. People are whispering that you might even take bribes from foreign states, so haughty are your ways. Perialla, on the other hand, is a model of friendliness and charm to all she meets."

"But that's ridiculous," Diodora said.

Eunous sniffed loudly. "If how she treats me, and the other slaves, is any indication, I know who I'd believe."

It was a painful period, coming to terms with what Perialla had done in taking Kleomenes' bribe, and how she felt about it. In her own mind we were at fault, not she; she hated us for thinking she'd done wrong—and she was going to make sure she punished us for it. But I've known much greater pain, and lived through it.

I hadn't known quite how to feel when I fell pregnant, back when I was sixteen. It was only afterwards that I understood what it would feel like to hold the baby.

My husband, Strepsiades, was delighted at my pregnancy: he was sure the child in my belly would be a strong son who would grow up to tend the family farm and carry on the family name. After all, that was my purpose: to breed sons for him. As well as that, of course, I was expected to manage his household: the spinning and the weaving, storing up the farm's produce, the eternal cooking, and caring for his flock of ducks, while he managed the orchard and the goats. The female slaves were hard-working and well-trained, thank the gods. They did all the real work around the house with little guidance from me, even reminding me when someone ought to feed the ducks, or check for eggs, or make a start on the evening meal.

Much of the time I sat and looked into the fire, or at the clouds scudding through the sky. The slaves warned me when their master was nearby, so that I could at least pretend to be a virtuous young wife. Wondering at my swelling belly, I felt quite dazed as I weighed out the wool for them to spin or weave, or told them what to cook. I'd been brought up for this, trained all my life for nothing but this endless woman's work, but now that it was happening, none of it felt real. I was lost in this new farm, half a day's walk from my father's house. My parents and their slaves and sheep could have been as far off as the moon.

My father brought my mother to my new home, once, in the horse-cart. I ran to Father with such joy; he was the only person who'd ever understood much of what I thought and said. He stepped back, his face serious, and said, "You are a wife, now, Thrasulla. Tell your slaves to bring wine to the andron for Strepsiades and me. We will talk of manly things. Take your mother indoors, and sit with her, like a good woman."

Chapter Twelve—Harmonia, The Slave

AFTER THE KUKEON, THE LENTILS, AND the long sleep, I felt like a new person—but Eukarpia was still coughing, and, in the morning light, whether I wanted to or not, I could see small red spots over her lips and tongue. I sat beside her pallet and prayed to Apollo the Healer to cure her. Perhaps I should have also prayed to the gods of our mother, from distant Thrace—but if they had any power here in Hellas, why were she and I slaves of the Athenians? The gods of Olympos are too strong for them to fight.

Reluctantly, I left Eukarpia on her pallet. She murmured as I went, but I don't think she even knew that I was leaving her alone. At least, I hoped that this was true.

I went to the kitchen for a chunk of barley bread and a few olives—I understood, now, that I wouldn't be able to look after anyone if I was weak from hunger—and walked along the colonnade to the boy's sickroom. Dosis was bent over him. She looked at me as a girl drowning in a pool might look at a branch held over the water. "Can you take over?" she asked. "Or at least help me? The master said you would, if you were well enough today."

I beckoned her to the doorway. Once we were both outside, I whispered, "How is he?"

"Worse, I think," Dosis said. "I feel so *helpless*. The mistress was with me for most of the night, but when she left me alone with him, I felt useless. How in the name of all the gods do you know what to *do*?"

"There's not much you can do," I said. "Keep him cool, keep the ulcers clean, give him water, feed him some thin barley porridge, if he can swallow it, and hold the bowl when he vomits it back up."

She pursed her lips wryly. "That's exactly what I've been doing. He says it's not the same as when you do it."

I couldn't help smiling at that, but then the tears started. Poor Aristogeiton. Oh, and poor Eukarpia. I sniffed them back, though, before Dosis could notice.

"He's just used to having me around," I said, trying to cheer her up. "I was there when he was born."

I'll never forget Aristogeiton's birth. He was only the second baby I ever saw born, and, like the first time, the screaming and the blood made my heart beat fast with fear. Pauson had promised a lamb to Artemis, Apollo's sister, protector of women in childbirth, if Ismenia produced a healthy heir, but I was still terrified for the mistress. I knew too well what had happened to my own poor mother in childbed. Men are said to be the courageous sex, but giving birth can be just as deadly as going off to war. When women die while giving birth, their clothes are dedicated to the goddess. Artemis' sanctuary is full of the clothes of women who died in childbed.

Ismenia was still only a girl when she birthed Aristogeiton, but she pushed him bravely out into the light of day. When it was over, she was triumphant at producing a lusty male heir at last, after the baby girl Philinna, and two miscarriages.

I pray to Apollo's virgin twin that I will never have to go through the ordeal of giving birth. Thank the gods, though, the possibility recedes each year, as I grow older. Athenian men like their women young, just as they like their boys. At twenty-two, I am six or seven years older than a girl thought ripe for marriage here.

But, right now, there were more pressing issues. "All right," I said to Dosis, "Let's have a look at the boy's ulcers together. They're the worst problem, I think."

Dosis screwed her nose up in good-natured disgust, and we opened the door to the boy's room. But he wasn't lying in his bed—he was standing up, naked and moaning, pouring water from the big pot of clean water by his bedside into his mouth and over his body. Weeping ulcerations covered his skin, and he was so thin that all his ribs were sticking out like a stray dog's.

"Harmonia—thank the gods you're here—I'm so *hot*," he shouted when he saw me. "You've got to do something to help me. I'm dying of thirst. I keep dreaming of throwing myself into our well. I know it would be stupid, but it would be so cool and so *wet*. I can't stand this much longer. I'm burning up inside. And I'm starving, but every time I eat something, I have to throw it straight up again."

Was this going to happen to my poor sister, too?

"Oh, sweetie, baby, just lie down on the bed, please," I said. Standing up wouldn't do him any good at all, only weaken him more. I walked cautiously towards him—he looked desperate enough to do anything—and took him by one hand. Even his fingers were oozing with foul liquids from burst ulcers.

"It's vile," he said, trying to pull his hand out of mine. I could see he was fighting back tears. He bent over, then, and coughed from the depths of his congested lungs.

"Come on, sweetie," I said, pulling Aristogeiton gently towards his bed. Hesitantly, he went to lie down again, but just in time I saw that the blanket on the bed was wet and stained with blood and worse. "Just stand there for a moment, baby," I said to him, and pulled the filthy blanket off the bed's thin mattress. I turned to point to the chest in the corner, but Dosis was already scuffling in there for a fresh blanket, which she smoothed quickly over the bed. "The third one since yesterday," she said, quietly.

Aristogeiton lay down, still coughing, and I poured the last of the clean water from the pot into a cup for him, handing the empty pot to Dosis to refill from the deep well in the courtyard. She scurried to the door with it, obviously relieved to have an errand that took her out of the sickroom.

As soon as she was gone, huge tears rolled down the boy's ulcerated face.

"Oh, Harmonia, I'm so hot, and everything hurts so much. I just want to die."

"Sweetie—"

"I *am* dying, aren't I? I can't forget the way that awful doctor looked at me yesterday—like a bad piece of meat in a butcher's shop, something from an animal that was sacrificed days earlier and isn't fit to eat anymore."

Snot was running down the boy's face, now, mixing with the blood and pus from the ulcers. I found a clean cloth, and wiped his face as gently as I could. It hurt me to do it. I could feel how painful the weeping ulcerations must have been for him.

All I could do was lie to him, again. "Aristogeiton, of *course* you're not dying. I told you that yesterday. You'll get better in a few days. You'll learn to recite every single book of the *Iliad* and the *Odyssey* at school, and how to wrestle and throw the javelin. You'll train as an ephebe, when you turn eighteen, so that you can fight all the enemies of Athens, especially the Spartans."

He didn't look convinced. I tried harder: "Um, and you'll become a sculptor, just like your father. You and your slaves will carve herms, and altars, and statues, and all sorts of things. Some of your work might even be used on the Akropolis, like those two big friezes your father carved for the new temple of Athena Parthenos."

I would never see Perikles' huge temple of Athena from close up—slaves were not allowed through the gates of the Akropolis—but the friezes Pauson had made had been magnificent. If it was all like that, it must be almost as splendid as Zeus' palace high on Mount Olympos.

He shook his head. "It's not going to happen, Harmonia. I'm trying to be brave, but it's too hard. I'm burning up inside. The fever is like fire in all my bones. I can't stand it much longer."

Dosis opened the door, then, carrying the big jug full now of cool water from the well, and a handful of clean cloths. I poured some of the water into a bowl and dipped a cloth in it. As carefully as I could, I dabbed gently at Aristogeiton's ulcerated face until it was all clean. The boy's teeth were gritted, and now and then he winced, despite himself. It felt like a knife going through my stomach.

I'd worked my slow and painful way down to the boy's emaciated

71

belly, and Dosis was carefully wiping at his feet and ankles, when Pauson came in. He bent over and kissed his son's poor, pitted, oozing forehead. "I brought you a honey-cake," he said to Aristogeiton, putting it on his pillow. "We need to fatten you back up." He smiled, but his voice came close to cracking as he said it.

Aristogeiton smiled up at his father. But how could he swallow even a crumb of cake, with his tongue and throat a bleeding mass of pain?

I beckoned Pauson to follow me out of the room. He closed the door, looking at me warily.

"Master," I said, "please forgive me for asking this, but do you think it would be a good idea to get the doctor to look at Aristogeiton again? The fever is getting worse. I could run to the doctor's house to ask, if you'd like me to, if you want to stay with him."

I didn't want to say aloud what I feared about my sister, but if the doctor came to the house, I would ask Pauson to let him see Eukarpia as well. Surely he would say yes . . .

Pauson put both hands up to his head and rubbed his scalp until his hair was a tangled mess. "I don't want the boy to hear," he said, very quietly. "I called in to the doctor's house this morning. The man who came here yesterday has taken to his bed, sick with the plague, and so has his slave."

Chapter Thirteen—Thrasulla, The Priestess

IN MY DISAPPOINTMENT AT BEING DISMISSED by my father, I barely heard a sentence of the hours of advice my mother gave me. No doubt it was *good* advice; she'd borne four children, and three of us had lived to adulthood. Her weaving was the envy of her friends, and none in her family had ever gone cold or poorly-dressed. She was the model of a dutiful wife and mother.

But I could hear Father in the fine andron with my husband, talking and laughing. I wanted so much to be there with Father, talking of politics and war, or health and disease, and even of my coming baby. Instead, I had my mother. She was more pleased with me than I'd ever seen her, except perhaps on the day of my wedding. I was a proper woman now, not the strange child who said things that made everyone uncomfortable. I'd given up seeking her approval before I was ten years old; I'd heard her whispering about me far too many times.

That day, I could not tell my mother how I felt, or didn't feel, about the coming baby. How could I disappoint her, when she was finally so pleased with me? Even if it was for something in which I'd had no volition. Instead, I let my mind wander while she tried to tell me how the birth would be. She did her best; she always did her best. But for all the sense she made to me, she might as well have been speaking the language of the Egyptians who live on the River Nile.

I cried all night, after my parents left the farm—our farm. Strepsiades said, "You miss them. It's only natural." But it was more than that.

Months later, when the birth pains started, I still felt strange, detached from everything around me. I'd seen sheep birthing all my life,

73

but I still could not believe a new life would emerge from my own swollen belly. It didn't feel like part of me at all. When the baby came at last, three days of torture later, she was cold and blue, already in the realm of Hades and his dark queen. All my prayers and promises to Artemis, the virgin huntress, my Lord Apollo's shining twin, had failed. The goddess whose realm it is to assist women in childbed had ignored me; perhaps she left me to her brother's mercy. The cord, knotted around my baby daughter's neck, had strangled her.

The midwife and my slaves curled my baby's tiny body into a terracotta pot; my husband buried her in the family plot near the road, where his father and mother already rested, with his dead siblings and innumerable slaves. She would not be lonely there, Strepsiades said, trying in his farmer's way to comfort me. That made me sob even louder. He sighed, and left the room. No one had taught this thirty-year-old farmer to cope with such a thing.

To my dismay, I could not even join the funeral procession for my own child. I could not stand for many days, or walk more than a few paces for several months. Something had torn within me during the long, slow, pain-filled birth, and I bled so much that I almost joined my baby in the small plot by the road. The midwife slept on a pallet next to my bed for days. When the bleeding finally stopped, she told me that another child brought to term would kill me and the child.

"She's an old fool," Strepsiades shouted, when he heard the news. "Just a stupid farmer's wife, an ignorant busy-body. What would she know?" My husband asked all of his friends, and even strangers in the marketplace, to help him find a real doctor, a male, who would of course know far more about the workings of the female body than a woman who'd helped birth a thousand babies in her long lifetime.

In time, a doctor came, examined me inside and out, asked many questions. Fortunately, the man my husband had found was not a fool. He shook his head, and said that there was nothing he could do. The midwife had been right. Another pregnancy would mean my death, and no live child.

My husband ranted furiously for a day or two, blaming me, my parents, and the Fates. How could the gods have cheated him like this?

74

His chosen wife, a strapping girl of sixteen, was barren now for life? It wasn't fair, or just. Had the gods not enjoyed the fragrant smoke from the many sacrifices he had made over the years? The sheep, and the piglets, and once, even a calf?

But when Strepsiades finally stopped shouting, he sat me down alone with him, and said that he would not divorce me, and take a more fertile wife. I thought then, and still suspect, that he could not bear the thought of giving my father back my handsome dowry, if he sent me back to my childhood home. As well as that, I've since come to understand, he'd grown fond of me in the months that we'd been married, even if I was by no means flawless as the mistress of his household. I'd always tried to keep my tongue restrained around him, not saying the kind of things that had made my mother and her slaves look at me strangely. It seems that it had worked; he liked to have me there, around his house. He still visited his friends, of course, and they visited him, carousing late in the andron, avoiding the rooms where we women worked and slept. But more and more, as time went on, my husband liked to sit in the courtyard with me at sunset, with a cup of wine, and talk over the small events of his day, or mine.

Strepsiades was kind to me, in his way, after the doctor made his sad pronouncement. From that day on, he stayed out of my bed. Instead, he worked his way through all the female slaves until he found the one he liked the best, and made her his concubine.

I didn't protest; it was his right. Even if I'd felt strong jealousy over this man I scarcely knew, master of my life, what could I have done? I did not wish to take him to my bed, whatever pleasure it might have given him and me, then die in agony after ten months had passed—and not even produce a healthy baby in the process.

Glukera was not unhappy to warm my husband's bed. He gave her lighter duties in the house, and even made her some small payment every month, with which one day she might buy her freedom. When she fell pregnant, his joy was tempered by a little fear; he knew now that a child of his might be a girl, or might even die still-born. But the baby, when he came, was a sturdy boy.

Strepsiades could have sold the boy, or exposed him. But instead, he treated the boy as if he'd come from his wife's legitimate womb. He decorated the front door with olive branches, and when the time came, he took the child into the family, parading him around the household hearth and naming him Kinesias after his own father.

A few days later, he held the proper feast for all his friends and relatives, even my parents, hiring a man to sacrifice a full-grown sheep. After the sacrificer-cook slit the sheep's throat and let the beast's blood pour over the small altar in our courtyard, he sliced up the animal on the table he'd brought with him, removed the skin, and wrapped long bones and other morsels in fat to burn on the altar as the gods' rightful portion. We prayed that all the gods would enjoy the smoke, as the sacrificer-cook poured unmixed wine over the flames.

Next, the man cut up the best of the animal's insides, the heart, the spleen, the kidneys and the tender liver, and slid them onto iron skewers. They went on the altar to roast as special treats for the guests of honor. While they were on the flames, the sacrificer-cook skillfully butchered the remaining carcass, cutting the muscle meat into chunks and setting them to boil in a tripod cauldron, with onions, herbs and barley. Slaves mixed great bowls of wine with water, and served it out to all, while we waited for the meat to stew.

I was not sad, during this merriment. The gods had willed my childless state; it seemed to fit, somehow, with my odd ways of thought. I'd been a distant, unsatisfactory daughter to my mother, a constant source of discontent to her. Perhaps it was better that one like me did not bring up a child. Perhaps . . .

Glukera sat her baby boy on my childless lap, and his starfish hands grasped for my empty breasts. I gently disengaged his tiny hands and gave him my gold bangle instead. He made a soft noise, bringing the bright bangle to his mouth, and Glukera smiled at me. I nodded; it was good. When Kinesias grew to adulthood, he and his future wife would tend the family graves, giving the dead the oil, milk and honey that was their due, as I did now. My own dead baby would not go hungry, down there in the dark earth.

Chapter Fourteen—Harmonia, The Slave

EVEN THE DOCTOR AND HIS SLAVE had the plague? Bile ran into my mouth. What could I do now if—as I feared—my sister had the same illness? How could I bear to live, if Eukarpia died?

"Perhaps the doctor who saw him first, master?"

The line between my master's eyes deepened. "He is already dead. That's why I called in the second one, pompous fool that he was. I wish I hadn't."

I understood. "Or another one?" My stomach clenched.

"After I heard that both of the doctors in our neighborhood were sick or dead, I asked around in the agora. I was desperate to find a doctor for my son, anywhere."

"Did you find one?"

All I could see on Pauson's face was despair. "If there is a doctor in Athens who is not dead or dying, no one can find him."

Tears welled in my eyes; I couldn't help it. Pauson may have thought that my tears were for Aristogeiton, and in part they were, but mostly for my twin, if she turned out to have the plague.

"Even if a doctor could be found," Pauson said, "I couldn't let you out of the front door alone. You haven't been outside since Aristogeiton got sick, have you?"

I shook my head.

"It's terrible out there," he said. "Sick people are staggering around in the streets, and crowding around the public fountains trying to get to water. We're so lucky to have a good, deep well here . . . But so many people have died, and with all the refugees from Attika crammed into

Athens, even in the temples—" he ran his hands over his face "—there are bodies everywhere, rotting in the sun."

"Oh," I said.

Pauson looked even more serious, if that were possible. "And some of the men who aren't sick are worse. They're not afraid of anything. They're raping and looting out there, worse than the Spartan army. It's anarchy."

No doctor would be able to come to see my sister. "It was a stupid idea," I said.

Pauson almost smiled. "It was a good idea, Harmonia. It's just that things out there are worse than you knew." His face grew sad again. "And maybe the gods wish it so. The men in the agora are talking about two oracles from Apollo at Delphi. One of them's an old verse that they say went like this: 'A Dorian war will come and with it plague,' though some people say the word wasn't plague, *loimos*, but famine, *limos*. Plague has to be the right word, though. The Spartans are Dorians, and they've certainly brought plague to the city, even if they didn't poison the reservoirs. We're not out fighting them, but we're dying like flies from this disease that came here with them."

I nodded, miserably. Like flies, indeed.

He said, "And the other oracle is much worse. Sometimes it seems that the priests and priestesses of Apollo in Delphi are on the side of the Spartans. The answers from the Pythia seem to favor the Spartans, not us, time after time."

I waited in silence. The master had so much on his mind.

"Before this conflict started," Pauson said at last, "the Spartans asked Apollo, at Delphi, whether they should go to war with us. The Pythia replied that if they fought with all their might, victory would be theirs, and the god himself would be on their side."

"Oh," I said. "Apollo Far-shooter, on their side." It was like a hard blow to my head. I could not read or write, but Ismenia could. She often read the *Iliad* out loud to her daughter while we slaves worked, and we were allowed to listen in. In the first book, the deadly arrows of Apollo bring plague to the Greek army when the god wants to punish them for maltreating his priest's daughter.

And, now, Apollo's own oracle at Delphi had said that the god was on the Spartan's side. Had he shot his arrows of plague at us, the Spartans' enemies?

"Yes," my master said, rubbing at his eyes, then looking straight at me. "It's too terrible to think about. If Apollo Far-shooter is on the Spartans' side, who then will heal us? Is our Athena strong enough to overcome Apollo?"

Aristogeiton died that night, while I was trying to rest at my sister's side, on Pauson's orders. As soon as I heard the wailing I knew what must have happened, but I couldn't bear to leave Eukarpia. Her tongue and throat were badly ulcerated, now, and her cough was painful to hear. Now and then she moaned, when she thought I was asleep. It was not a summer cold. I couldn't deny it any longer, even to myself. But perhaps Apollo would spare her, even if he was on the side of Athens' enemies. My sister and I were slaves, mere chattels, not true Athenians by birth.

My mistress Ismenia came to my bed at mid-morning, telling me to help her to lay out her son for burial. Her lovely face was haggard with grief. Wet tracks of tears ran down her reddened cheeks.

"I need you with me now, Harmonia," my mistress said, almost pleading, as I stumbled to my feet and pulled my tunic into decent shape. "I trust you. You've been here with me ever since I left my father's house to marry Pauson. Ktema will help as well, but I need you." Her voice was harsh with wailing through the night.

I looked at my mistress, then down at my sister coughing on her pallet. In the dawn light, I could see red pustules forming on Eukarpia's face and chest.

"Is it . . . ?" Ismenia said, the sorrow on her face overlaid with a new worry.

"I think so," I whispered.

Ismenia walked over to Dosis' pallet, and shook her awake. "Dosis," the mistress said, "wake up. I know you were up late with me and my son last night, but Eukarpia is sick."

Dosis sat up slowly, rubbing the sleep out of her eyes. She looked terrible.

Ismenia said, "Your main task today is to look after Eukarpia. If anyone asks you to do anything else, tell them to come to me. Do anything you can to make Eukarpia more comfortable. Is that clear?"

Dosis nodded.

The mistress added, "But try to get some rest as well, if you can. I don't want you getting sick too."

Of course I would have preferred to stay with my sister, but Dosis was sensible for her age. She had been good with Aristogeiton, though she'd lacked confidence in her skills—and Eukarpia would be comfortable with her. Most of all, though, how could I have refused my mistress, who had just lost her son and heir?

And so, Dosis sat with my twin, instead of me, while Ktema and I helped the mistress through the prescribed rituals, and the boy's sister, Philinna, watched and wept for him. Ktema knew exactly what had to be done. In her long life, she'd dealt with many births, and so many deaths.

First she filled a special pot with water from our neighbor's cistern, untainted by death, and placed it at the door; passers-by, seeing it, would know there'd been a death within, and anyone who left the house could use the water to purify themselves. After that, the old slave led Ismenia and me step by sorrowful step, showing us how to wash the boy's body and scent it with perfumed oil, dress it in clean white clothes, then lay it on a light bed, in the courtyard, with olive branches looped and tied as a garland for his head, and his feet facing the door. We worked almost in silence.

Moody Kalonike came out of her room at last, watching us like a vulture as we washed and dressed Aristogeiton's bone-thin, ulcer-covered corpse. She wailed and wept like a madwoman, mourning the nephew she'd scarcely spoken to while he was still alive, and never once visited on his sickbed. She took ashes from the hearth and rubbed them on her face and hair, and clung onto her niece Philinna, who cringed away from her.

When no one paid Kalonike any mind—Ismenia and I were too busy following Ktema's careful instructions as to how the ritual should proceed—she got a knife from the kitchen and hacked at her lustrous dark hair, cutting it shorter than any slave's. She bullied poor Philinna into holding up the ornate bronze hand-mirror for her.

Still, we took no notice of the woman's excesses. We knew from bitter experience that it would only send our master's sister into more violent frenzies.

Enraged at being ignored, Kalonike grabbed at Ismenia's arm and screamed, "Why do you not cut your hair like a proper mother, you slut? Why do you not tear your clothes to rags? Do you care so little that my brother's child is dead? Unnatural bitch!"

Philinna cowered away from her aunt, and my mistress winced, her swollen eyes even redder than before. "My husband does not wish me to cut my hair," she said quietly. "Ask him about it, if you wish. You have the right; you are his sister."

After that, Ismenia kept her head down, doing her best to ignore her sister-in-law while she got on with the work of preparing her son's body for burial.

At Ktema's prompting, I fetched the boy's favorite toys from his storage chest—the spinning top, the hoops, the set of knuckle-bones—and the stylus and waxed tablet he'd used at school, and placed them around his half-skeletal body.

The rituals came back to me as we performed them. The previous year, while we were walled up here in Athens for the first time, the mistress had had a baby son die of a summer fever soon after he'd taken his first steps. Just like this time, we'd washed and perfumed him and dressed him beautifully.

Before dawn, the funeral procession had carried the little corpse, and the amphora his father had bought to place him in, through the Dipylon Gate in the pottery district. Men and women the master had hired had walked along with us, holding flaming torches and playing the double flute. The amphora was buried in the hole the men had dug beside the Sacred Way to Eleusis, in Pauson's family plot.

We'd visited the baby's grave at the right times, poured oil, honey, wine and milk into the soil beside the marble marker, and left barley cakes to nourish Ismenia's son. Soon, Aristogeiton would be buried near that small boy, his brother.

The master came in from the street just as Ktema put a honey-cake beside Aristogeiton's body, to go into the soil with him as an offering to the gods of the underworld. Pauson held the small, white-painted jar that he'd gone to the agora to buy. It, too, would be buried with the boy, full of scented oil.

"I was lucky to get this," he said to us. His eyes were red, and the bags under them were huge. "There were hardly any left anywhere in the city." He sighed. "Too many people have died in the city this last month. Even the potters and the painters have fallen ill."

Chapter Fifteen—Thrasulla, The Priestess

I KNOW IT WASN'T me, or Diodora, who let the secret out that Kleomenes had bribed Perialla and Kobon. I don't know who it was; but *someone* in Sparta knew too much, whether it was a friend of Kleomenes who knew the truth and had turned on him, or whether a too-lucky guess had found its guilty mark. Our net of helpful eyes and ears told us the rumor had first been whispered in one of the Spartan soldiers' clubhouses, over a meal of black broth and wild game, and had spread through Laconia like wild-fire.

At any rate, sooner or later, one of the Spartiates accused Kleomenes out loud, in the marketplace. He could have bluffed, and denied everything. Who, after all, could prove such a thing? But half-mad as he was, impious Kleomenes told the tragic truth: he had corrupted the Pythia, and dishonored Apollo. Before he could be punished by the Spartan state as it saw fit, he took fright and fled to Thessaly.

They say that good news stays at home, but bad news travels fast. In a few days, the news about Kleomenes' confession and flight had spread through every tiny hamlet in all Hellas, and probably beyond, to Persia and Egypt. And, with the truth about the king, came the truth about the Pythia he'd bribed.

Perialla tried to brave it out, at first. After all, she'd thoroughly convinced herself that she was in the right. In her own mind, she'd done no wrong by taking the king's gifts—in fact, she'd honored Lord Apollo by coming before him more richly arrayed. But something was said to her at one of those fine lunches she attended, and she returned whey-faced and weeping. According to our slaves, who asked *their* slaves, Aristophantos' wife, Kobon's wealthy mother, had snubbed the Pythia when she'd entered the house. That might have been mere accident, but then Kobon's stupid wife had touched Perialla's earring while commenting on Kleomenes' taste in gold, and everyone had laughed. Perialla had laughed too, but not for long. The women froze her out, more savage than wolves with their own kind. Before the meal was served, the Pythia scuttled back home alone.

It may have been the darkest day of Perialla's life. When I glimpsed her in the shaded colonnade at the side of the courtyard, the next day—she could not hide from me forever, sharing the house, hard though she tried—she'd aged ten years at least. Her hair was not just grey, but thin and lank, the skin sagged on her face and throat, and her eyes were shot with blood.

"It's all your fault," she said, her voice bitter as year-old vinegar. "You whispered around Delphi that Kleomenes had made me gifts."

I shook my head. "Never."

She spat onto the courtyard floor. "I know the truth. You cannot hide from me. I was Pythia before you, and will be Pythia still when you are dead. It was you."

"No."

"And Kobon's wife—why has she come out of this unscathed? Why is she not accused like me?"

"I don't know."

It didn't matter what I said, after that. She was almost as mad as Kleomenes by then, though her eyes were red, and not, like his, unnaturally bright.

Before the next day of the oracle, our slaves warned us that Apollo's priests were coming in a delegation to our house. The slaves had heard it from the priests' slaves before dawn, while they were all fetching water at the nymph's spring. Perialla ignored us when we asked her to come out of her room, so Diodora and I waited nervously without her, in the andron. Diodora had a spindle in her hand for comfort, and I had a basket of washed wool to pull out into workable pieces, but we were too worried to do any useful work. However events unfolded that day, we knew they would not be good.

When the sun was high in the faded blue sky of dusty summer, the priests knocked at the outer door of our house, and Eunous brought them to us. We'd worked for years with each of them in the temple of Apollo; they were good men, if limited by the prejudices common to those brought up in wealthy households. Gorgias, the most senior of the priests, was at their head.

"The Spartan Ephors have sent messengers to us," Gorgias said, after the lengthy formal greetings that the men seemed to think were necessary. "Kleomenes has confessed to gross impiety: using Kobon of Delphi as intermediary, he corrupted a Pythia with gifts."

The bribery was official, now, not merely rumor. The priests had to act.

I said, "You bring us news of a terrible thing."

Gorgias said, "Kobon of Delphi gave clothes and jewelry to Perialla, on Kleomenes' behalf, in order that she would pronounce Demaratos illegitimate while sitting on Apollo's mantic tripod, under his holy temple. It is suspected that her reply to the question put to her by the Spartan sacred messengers was not inspired by the god."

"I fear you are correct," I said. "It is a great violence done to the god whom we all serve."

"There is more bad news," the spokesman said. He sounded genuinely distressed. "Demaratos fled east, after the false oracle was made known in Sparta by the sacred messengers, and he was believed illegitimate. Now he has sent to the Spartans to tell them that, in their foolishness, they created a fearsome enemy to Hellas. What he has done is hardly to be comprehended by a true Hellene."

"Tell us, Gorgias." I was fairly sure what the bad news was going to be.

"The former king of Sparta took refuge with the Persian king."

"That's bad indeed." Diodora and I had expected this, and had heard some rumors that Persia was Demaratos' goal when he left Sparta.

It was only natural that one so badly used would seek his country's enemy.

Demaratos claimed royal descent, and could expect the rulers of Persia to greet him kindly. We could not say so, to the innocent priests. They could never understand the murk and pain that lies within men's breasts, that forces them to act in ways they'd otherwise despise. Nevertheless, Demaratos' defection was still an act of treachery to his motherland. I made the face of one disgusted, and it was not all play-acting.

The priest went on: "We heard the worst in secret, late last night: King Darius welcomed Demaratos with open arms. Why would he not? Demaratos is a seasoned soldier and a great strategist, who knows the strengths and weaknesses of all the city-states of Hellas. Darius has given him lands and wealth. Demaratos now rules three cities that once were Lydian: Pergamon, Teuthrania, and Halisarna. He will be a powerful ally for the Persian king."

My belly had been roiling with anxiety for Perialla; now it was cold with fear for Hellas as a whole. We hadn't heard that news. "This is a sad day for all Hellenes," I said, and Diodora nodded mutely. The Persian threat was stronger now. How could tiny Hellas hold out against the might of the greatest empire the world had ever seen?

The priest looked grave. "Aristophantos, Kobon's father, was at the meeting where we heard this news. By midnight he had sent Kobon away, before he could be exiled from Delphi." The priest's companions were murmuring quietly amongst themselves. It seemed they were not sorry to see Kobon gone from their town.

"It is a fitting punishment," I said. Kobon would strut our streets no more, proud of his father's wealth and his own high influence. He would be a nobody, nowhere, from now on.

Gorgias, most senior of the priests, looked at me then. There was desperation in his eyes, but his voice was stern. "We must ask you this, Thrasulla: bring the corrupted Pythia to us, for Apollo's sake."

The hairs lifted at the back of my neck, my head snapped up, and the god spoke through me, even though I was not seated on the bronze tripod under his temple. "Perialla is no longer a Pythia."

The priests could tell who spoke with my mouth. They raised their hands to the heavens. "It shall be as Apollo wills."

My body mine again, I asked, "What will you do with her?" There were some possibilities I could not stomach being part of.

Gorgias held out his open hand to me. "She will not be harmed. She will be taken back to her family in Krisa, a plain woman again, and not a Pythia."

I nodded. It would be worse than death for her, with her desperate desires, but it was not needlessly cruel. "That's a fitting punishment. But I cannot fetch Perialla for you. She has been suspicious, and has refused to do anything we ask. But you may try, with the authority of Apollo."

Gorgias beckoned to two strong young servants of the god. "Take us to her room now, please, Thrasulla."

Chapter Sixteen—Harmonia, The Slave

PAUSON HELD THE LITTLE OIL-JAR out to his wife. The painting on its white background was delicate and strangely intimate: a family visiting a grave, carrying food and drink for a dead child, just as we would visit Aristogeiton.

Ismenia looked at it and burst into tears. I wanted to sob, myself, but I bit my lip as hard as I could bear. This was a day for her sorrow, not for mine.

Pauson put an arm around his wife and went on talking, faster and faster.

"The other oil-jars were no good. Oh, there was a one with a picture of a soldier going off to war, that Aristogeiton would have liked, I think, but he was so young. And there were some nice ones with people waiting on the banks of the Styx for Charon to bring his ferry over to them. One of them even had Hermes Psychopompos waiting with them on the banks of the Styx, ready to escort them onto the ferry. But the people were all too old. There wasn't much for a boy our son's age. But this is nice," he said, holding the jar out again for Ismenia to see. "He'll know we will come to visit him."

Ismenia sobbed and sobbed. Pauson looked quite helpless. "I've got a lovely stele for Aristogeiton's grave in the workshop," he said. "It's a boy our son's age with a dog. He always wanted a dog." By this time the tears were running down my face; I couldn't help it. Eventually, Ktema took the oil jar from Pauson's hand, and put it near the boy's head.

Pauson gave Ktema a look of thanks, and led his wife towards their bedroom. She didn't stop crying, but she didn't resist.

"Come, Ismenia," he said to her. "You must rest a little. You had no sleep at all last night." Then, over his shoulder, he said to me, "Harmonia, could you bring some honeyed wine for my wife? Or whatever you think best. She must be strong for the funeral tonight."

"Don't worry, brother," Kalonike said, loudly. "I will wail by the corpse all day, as is right and proper for the women of his family."

I thought I saw Pauson shudder as he walked away.

Pauson and Ismenia would leave the house before dawn, I knew, with torch-bearers and musicians, if the master could find any to hire amongst all the death in Athens. But I could not go to the grave with them this time. How could I leave my sister, while she was sick, and perhaps dying?

After I took the cup of honeyed wine to my mistress—she was prostrate on the marital bed, crying her eyes out—Ktema sent me up to my sister.

"I'll stay here," she said. "I'll call you if you're needed, don't worry. But, from what I've seen, she needs you more than anyone else."

My sister, my twin, my only true family, died eight days later. There were the necessary purifying rituals to cleanse us from Aristogeiton's death, but, apart from them, I spent the whole time at my sister's side, bathing her ulcerated flesh with cool, clean water, feeding thin barley porridge to her and catching it in bowls when she retched it up, and trying not to cry while she could see or hear me. I was so distraught that I could not have eaten a scrap of Aristogeiton's funeral feast even if I'd wanted to leave her side for it.

Nothing I did for my sister had helped. Eukarpia still died, burned up with fever and thin as a stray beast starving in the streets.

In the courtyard, in the mid-morning sun, Ismenia and I washed and anointed my sister's corpse for burial. I could hardly move: I felt as if one arm and leg had been cut off, and half my head.

That day, Ktema was sitting indoors with Philinna, who had a headache. Ismenia pretended not to worry that it was the plague, but her eyes were haunted. Kalonike stayed in her room; a slave's death was barely worth remarking. Both of her Syrian slaves were sick, now, but she left their care to Ismenia to organize. Dosis had been tending to them as well as she could, while also helping me with Eukarpia when I was too tired to move even for my sister.

"We'll bury your sister next to my son," Ismenia said when we were finished. "You'd like that, wouldn't you?" She smoothed down the clean white clothes we'd dressed Eukarpia in, and looked at me. I saw my mistress' expression change from pity to alarm.

"What's wrong?" I asked.

"It's your face, Harmonia. There are some little red spots on your face. They're tiny, but . . ." she said, trailing off. "How do you feel?"

I put my hands up to my cheeks and forehead. What my fingers touched made me feel sick to my stomach. While my sister had been dying, plague pustules had forced their way through my skin. I'd been coughing, but I'd thought I was just tired. Unwilling, I ran my tongue around the inside of my mouth, and found countless bleeding ulcers that I hadn't noticed in my misery over my sister. Perhaps I would join her soon, beneath the Earth.

Ismenia could see from my expression what I had discovered. "Go to bed, right now," she said. "I'll send someone to look after you. And I'll take care of your sister." Her voice was harsh, but I saw the tears roll down her face as she waved me away.

The next two weeks are a blur of grief, fever and pain. The pain and fever were kinder than the grief; when they receded far enough and I knew where I was and who I was, I knew also that my sister was not there with me, above the ground. She was down in Hades' kingdom, wandering without me, lost and alone. When those times came, I wished that I were dead, along with her.

However much I might have wished it, I didn't die from the fever, like Aristogeiton and my sister, or from the diarrhea that followed, like one of Kalonike's Syrian slaves. Dosis and Ktema nursed me, and Ismenia helped when their strength was exhausted. I have a few sharp memories of throwing up for painful hours, until my throat and stomach bled, and of voiding my bowels helplessly, in agony, but most of the time is mercifully blurred in my mind, like a bad dream that dissolves on waking.

Thanks to whatever god saved my life—perhaps Apollo the Healer, perhaps warlike Athena, perhaps my mother's unknown Thracian gods—the plague did not send me blind, or lame, or worse. I could no longer move the two smallest fingers on my left hand, but I could still spin, and clean, and cook almost as well as I had before.

By the time I could stand and work again, the Spartans had left Attika, and Kalonike had gone back home, thank the gods. It's hard to say which of the two the family was more thankful for. The useless woman's husband had returned to Athens unscathed, after ravaging the fields of Troezen under Perikles' leadership. Their son was home safe from war, as well; after the Spartans had left, they'd gone back to their farm near Plataia, with her baby daughter, all unharmed, and her surviving slave.

Ktema told me, with a sour expression, that Pauson had been forced to bury his sister's dead slave in his own plot. After ignoring both of them while they were sick, Kalonike hadn't cared enough about the one who died even to see her decently interred. Ismenia had prepared the corpse for burial with her own hands, with no help from her sister-in-law.

Chapter Seventeen—Thrasulla, The Priestess

As I led Gorgias and the servants of Apollo through the colonnade bordering the courtyard, I heard strange noises from Perialla's room. They sounded like an animal in pain.

The two young men knocked down Perialla's flimsy door in moments.

She sat cross-legged on the floor, rocking back and forth, and mewling like a puppy with a crushed paw. Her fine gold jewelry was in her lap; her bony hands clutched at the pieces, almost crushing them. She knew what was to happen.

The priest looked confused, and the servants of the god hung back outside the door.

"Come, Perialla," I said, and put out my hand towards her. "It is time. You must go with these men. They will take you to your home."

"It's not my fault," she said, and came up into a clumsy crouch. The jewelry fell from her lap onto the floor, and she scrabbled at it, without much success.

I found a thick cloak in her clothes chest, and wrapped the jewelry up in it securely. "Take this," I said, handing it to her. "It will be useful to you in the days to come."

I found another cloak, a lighter one, and wrapped it around her thin shoulders. "You'll need this, too," I said. The day was warm, but the cloak, pulled over her head, would help protect her from the vicious eyes and voices of the crowd.

I held her by one hand and led her from the room as if she were a scolded child taking her punishment. The fearsome woman who had been senior Pythia followed me without protest or argument, her face

92

empty. Gorgias looked on in wonder, his eyes as large as the bowls that wine is mixed in for a feast.

But it was not so strange. Perialla had been a Pythia, despite taking the bribe. She had denied her guilt, and laid the blame on us, but now that the time had come, she knew her fate. She could not escape it.

"Bring her chest of clothes," I said to the young men outside the door. "They should go with her."

A cart was waiting on the dry, gray road when I led Perialla from the house. Apollo's sunlight dazzled me, reflected from the Phaidriades, the shining cliffs that stand guard over his beloved town of Delphi. Tears streamed down Perialla's ruined face. I had to prize her fingers from my hand, one by one, before she would let go and climb into the cart. The young servants of Apollo sat up front, to drive the horse and gossip together on the long way down to Perialla's family's farm in Krisa, far below Delphi, towards the Gulf of Corinth. Their bodies shrank from her; she was a woman who had been touched by power, and now was empty.

Late summer dust, as dry as death, billowed behind the cart as it drove off.

Three months went by. Life returned to normal, if there was ever such a state as normal for the Pythiai of Apollo, waiting every month to be filled with the god. On the seventh of each month, Diodora and I descended again and again to the *adyton* of Apollo's temple, sat on the sacred tripod, and breathed the god's sweet vapors. We gave the best answers we could, with Apollo's help, to those who came with questions about matters large and small: city-states wanting advice about where to found a colony or whether to wage a war, citizens asking about crops to plant or marriages to make.

We chose a new trainee Pythia, along the way. Kleitagora was, like us, a woman over fifty, her husband dead, her children settled, not held too tightly by the bonds of family. Like us, too, her eyes and ears were sharp, and she thought far more than she spoke.

Kleitagora spun and wove with us, pretended like us to be a proper Hellene widow, as we sifted the news that our network brought to us:

the price of gold, the weather patterns, the pointless posturings of kings and politicians. The threat of mighty Persia hung over all Hellas, like the sword of Damokles ready to destroy it, if the warring Hellene states did not destroy one another first. But while we feared for Hellas' fate, we waited to hear the end of half-mad Kleomenes' story.

Chapter Eighteen—Harmonia, The Slave

WITH KALONIKE AND THE SPARTANS GONE, and Aristogeiton and my sister dead, our life went on. One day, Ismenia had the women in the courtyard, spinning and weaving, just as we used to do before the Spartans had come to Attika, and the plague followed them. The mistress was right to do it: her son was dead, and so was my sister, but those of us who remained above the Earth would still need clothes and blankets against the elements. Blazing summer was merging into autumn; winter would soon be upon us. We had to be prepared for the days when we would need a brazier burning in the room upstairs, to keep our fingers warm enough to work.

That day, Ktema, Dosis and I were spinning wool; Ismenia was weaving in the cool shade, with help from her daughter. Philinna watched her mother carefully, studying just what to do, and how. Too soon, she would be managing slaves of her own, weaving cloth for her own household. Her headache, back when I fell sick, had not been the plague, thank all the gods, but the onset of her periods. She was a woman now, and Pauson was looking around his friends for a good husband for her, a trustworthy man of thirty years or so who would be kind to her.

Ismenia said, quite suddenly, "Why is it so hot? It shouldn't be so hot, here in the shade. My head's so hot. Can someone get me a cup of cold water?" She shook her head, as if she was confused.

I looked at her, and looked away, worried and fearful; I saw Ktema do it too. Dosis stood quickly and walked to the well, muttering, "No, it cannot be," so softly that perhaps no one but me could hear her.

Philinna's face turned pale, and she stepped back until she found a chair to hold on to. "Mother," she said, "how do you feel?"

"Don't be silly, darling, it's not the plague, if that's what you're thinking," Ismenia said, draining the cup of water that Dosis handed her. "How could I have the plague? That would be stupid. I'm just so hot. Isn't everyone hot, today?"

Even in the sun it was quite cool, that day, and a chilly breeze was blowing from the sea.

"Yes, Mother," Philinna said, calmly. "It's *very* hot. We're all very hot. But maybe you should rest for a while, indoors, where it's cooler." She looked at Ktema for support.

Ktema turned her head to me and gave me an anguished look, but smoothed out her face and forced a smile on it before she turned back to her mistress. "Your daughter's right, mistress," she said. "You've been working without a break for days, weaving, and it's much too hot to work so hard. A little rest would do you good. Here, I'll take you to your bedroom and get you into bed. Harmonia, start making a kukeon for the mistress, will you? I'll come and help in a few minutes."

Ismenia started coughing before noon, and later that day Ktema found plague ulcers on her tongue. Our mistress died nine days later, of the fever.

Because I'd had the plague and lived through it, I was the one who nursed Ismenia, most of the time. Everyone said the same thing in the agora: no one who'd recovered from the disease could catch it again. I would have nursed her anyway, risking another dose of the foul illness, despite the misery of the retching and the runs. I would have welcomed death; it would have taken me straight to my sister's side without the need for poison, or a sharp blade.

But I continued to live, indifferent though I was, and Ismenia died. This time, Ktema and I laid out her body with young Philinna's help. Together we lamented the dead woman, as was her right, while we washed and anointed her corpse, dressing her in white and garlanding her head, and pointing her feet towards the door.

The funeral monument that Pauson chose for her was the loveliest

I'd seen come from his workshop, a marble stele carved with a woman taking jewelry from a box held out by a slave. It looked far too much like our mistress, and my sister, to be part of his standard stock—which was almost all gone, after so many deaths in Athens. He wouldn't talk about it, when I asked, but I believe that he despaired when she fell sick, and carved with his own hands a monument especially for her—and my sister.

Chapter Nineteen—Thrasulla, The Priestess

THE STORY OF KLEOMENES' END, when we heard it, was stranger than the works of poets, inspired by Apollo and the Muses.

As we'd been told before, he fled from Sparta into horse-breeding Thessaly, where he might have been safe from causing harm to anyone, even himself. Unfortunately, he didn't stay there; it seemed he quietly returned to Arcadia, just north of Sparta. Amongst the states of Hellas, neighbors are seldom friends. The important men of Arcadia had little reason to love the Spartans, and Kleomenes, with all his skills in manipulating men and women, worked first on one and then the next, binding them by strong oaths to attack Sparta along with him. Our people told us, strange to say, that he took the chief men of Arcadia to the city of Nonakris, near Pheneus, and made them swear allegiance to him by the water of the Styx.

The river of the dead rises to the surface of the Earth there in Arcadia; it's a small stream that falls down from a cliff into a walled pool. The dead are with us always, here in Hellas. It is fear of them, and fear of death, that so often brings men to harm.

The Spartans were afraid when they learned that Kleomenes was uniting the Arcadians against them. Against all reason, they persuaded him to go back to Sparta, and made him king again, just as before. Perhaps they thought it safer, with such a dangerous man, to have him on their side.

Soon after that, great men from Sparta came to Delphi, to sacrifice at Apollo's temple. They did not speak to us: we were mere women, even if we were Apollo's mouthpieces. But their slaves spoke with our slaves, and one came to our house. He told us the whole story.

No one, it seemed, other than us, had noticed Kleomenes' madness, back in his days of glory, or even in his scheming exile. Once he was back in Sparta, though, it was no longer secret: the old king poked his walking-stick into the face of any Spartiate that he met on the street. He was a king again, but even the behavior of a king has its limits. His relatives, long put-upon, bound his feet in stocks to keep him out of trouble. He raged like a rabid wolf until there was only a single guard, a helot, and no spectators.

Kleomenes, king of the Spartans, once one of the greatest of Hellenes, asked his helot guard for a knife. The guard said no, of course, but Kleomenes threatened him with the nameless punishments he would inflict when he was freed. The terrified guard gave the king a knife. What harm could Kleomenes do, even with a knife, fixed there in the stocks?

What happened next, only those who'd looked into those half-mad eyes could understand. Kleomenes took the knife from the helot. He set the point against his sandaled shin, and slashed up to the muscly thigh, then from the thigh to the hip and the sides of his royal body, until he reached his lean warrior's belly. The helot, by now, was wild with fear, but dared not stop the king.

Once Kleomenes reached his belly, he used the knife to cut the thin layer of flesh that lay over his guts into narrow strips. Loops of intestines pushed out between the ribbons of belly flesh; blood spurted and seeped and gushed. The king lost control of the knife he held. Soon afterwards, he died.

The Hellenes, always argumentative, could not decide which god had sent Kleomenes his dreadful death. Most said that Apollo had driven him mad for corrupting the Pythia here in Delphi. The Athenians said the death was sent because he'd invaded their most sacred town, Eleusis, and laid waste the precinct of the two goddesses, Demeter and Persephone. The Argives claimed that it was his impiety in their own state, when he'd attacked them; he'd burned a sacred grove down to the ground, and killed men who'd taken refuge there. Perhaps it was all of those acts, or none.

Most Spartans, abstemious to a fault in food and drink, said that Kleomenes went mad from the neat wine that the Skythian ambassadors had taught him to drink, when they came to Sparta to propose a joint attack on Persia. But that cannot be true; strong wine can lead a man to endless trouble, but not to Kleomenes' passionate lunacy. Some even said the fearful mutilation was a lie, an invention of the Spartan aristocracy, who'd murdered him and needed a story to covered up the facts. That made no sense: why would they have invented so strange a tale, when a simple stabbing in the heart would have been enough, and child's play for the soldier-king?

Chapter Twenty—Harmonia, The Slave

Autumn, 429BC

IN THE THIRD YEAR OF THE WAR with Sparta, Perikles died.

As usual, we women spent the morning spinning and weaving in the workroom upstairs. Philinna was weaving a new chiton on her mother's upright loom. The cloth that she was producing was good: not quite as skilled as her mother's, not quite so even and so densely packed, but more than serviceable, and improving every row. I was sure her next one would be better, as this was better than the one she'd made before. By the time she went in the noisy torchlit procession to her new husband's home, she would be a valuable asset to his household.

At noon we took a break, and went downstairs to the sunny courtyard to eat our lunch of barley bread and goat's cheese, with a few olives. As always, Ktema had carefully placed a piece of each onto the household altar, for the gods.

My master came with the news at noon; he'd heard it in the agora.

"Perikles is dead," Pauson said. "It will be the ruin of Athens."

I pitied the master more than the dead strategos, seeing him that day. Pauson's hair had grayed and thinned almost to nothing in the months after his wife and son had died, and the deep lines between his eyes and around his mouth were permanent now. When he walked, he moved like an old man. Despairingly, he said, "How can we defeat the Spartans without him at our head?"

"What's happened, husband?" the new mistress asked, coming out of the kitchen with a bowl of grapes.

Pauson repeated the news about the great strategos to his young wife, Nanno. "Perikles is dead. Some say it was the plague that killed him, others that his heart was broken."

She looked at him, confusion in her huge, brown eyes. "What would break a famous general's heart? Wasn't he too important for things like that?"

Pauson ran his fingers through his hair and looked indulgently at the girl. Nanno was barely older than his daughter, Philinna. At nearly fifty, he must have been more than three times his young wife's fifteen years. Nanno's father, Drakes, ran the weapons factory where Pauson's male slaves still worked, and often ate and drank with Pauson and his other friends in lavish dinner-parties, with pretty boys and girls to entertain them all until dawn. After Ismenia and Nanno's intended husband had both died of the plague, Drakes had proposed the match. It made sense to both of them: Pauson needed a male heir, now that Aristogeiton was dead, and Nanno needed a man before she was too old for marriage. All knew, as well, that Athens had to breed new hoplites against the Spartan threat.

Pauson said to the new mistress, "The assembly blamed Perikles for the war with Sparta, and for the plague, because he was the one who shut us up inside the walls. They stopped him being strategos, and even fined him, last winter. Do you remember that?"

She looked puzzled. "My father said something about that, I think. Yes, I remember."

"Even now, those who still blame him are dancing in the streets, drunk in full daylight, rejoicing at his death."

"You do not blame him, husband?" Nanno handed me the bowl of grapes that she'd been carrying, and put an arm out to Pauson.

"Death and disease come at the will of the gods," he said. "We mortals must endure them as best we can. But Perikles had endured too much, perhaps. He'd lost most of his family to the plague. His eldest son Xanthippos, who'd been estranged from him, died of it, and his sister, then his only remaining legitimate son, Paralos. After that, is it any wonder that Perikles got sick himself?"

She shook her head sadly. Was her sorrow for the death of the man she'd been engaged to, or for Pauson's lost wife and child? I didn't know her well enough to guess; perhaps it was for both.

Patiently, the master kept explaining: "It was the plague, they say, but not a normal dose of it. It usually kills within twelve days, but he was sick for months. Perhaps it really was a broken heart. He was our greatest statesman."

The mistress stroked Pauson's shoulder sympathetically. "He was an old man. He must have been so very tired, after everything that had happened."

She didn't say, "Like you." Perhaps she didn't even think the words, but Ktema and I looked at each other, appalled.

A wave of pain passed over Pauson's face and disappeared, leaving him looking merely weary. He said, slowly, "Yes, Nanno. I'm sure Perikles was tired, after everything. The war, the plague, his family—everything."

Chapter Twenty-one—Thrasulla, The Priestess

MY HUSBAND'S DEATH WAS SLOWER than Kleomenes', more ordinary, and far more cruel. When we'd been married thirteen years, Strepsiades sweated and shivered with cough and fever throughout a whole hot summer. Often the fever would leave him for a day, and he'd get out of bed, make plans to prune the olives or re-pasture the goats. The next day, though, the fever would come back stronger and more savage than ever. His hands and feet were ice and snow, while children ran around naked in the summer heat and dust.

The doctor, when he visited, looked grave. "It's an accumulation of phlegm and bile," he said to me outside the room. "They gather in the lungs, and form great lumps of pus. He'll try to cough them up. Pray to Apollo the Healer that he can. The Far-shooter's arrows bring disease, but he can heal men, if he chooses."

At first, my husband's flushed cheeks made him look healthy and fit, though he grew thinner all the time, hard muscle wasting slowly off his bones. Kinesias, his son by Glukera, was eleven years old now; he came after school each day to play board games with him. The tall, slim boy was sure his father would be well again before the end of autumn. I felt it in my guts, though, that this was not to be.

When winter came, Strepsiades could not even rest quietly in bed, between the bouts of shivering; his painful bowels had him out of bed, shouting and swearing in agony, all hours of the night and day. Before too long, he grew too weak to walk outside. We placed a bucket by the bed, which the slaves emptied and returned time and again. The doctor shook his head, when he saw that. "Not a good sign," he said. "Pray to Apollo."

Worst of all, though, was the coughing. In summer the cough had come in intermittent fits, but by winter it was constant. His throat was red as fire, and burnt like flame each time he struggled to bring up the pus-filled phlegm from his struggling lungs. His chest felt like a stone, he said. His throat was whistling like a flute when he breathed, his hair fell out, and he was coughing blood.

I called the doctor yet again. He saw my husband's hairless head, and threw some of his sputum on the fire. It smelled like burning flesh. The doctor took my arm and led me from the room, pursing his lips.

"There's no hope, now. It could be days, or weeks. Pray to Apollo that it is only days."

But Strepsiades lived far too long after that visit, coughing his lungs up night and day. I cried behind locked doors, knowing my husband's agony. If his farm beasts had been in pain like that, he would have given them an easy death. Apollo Far-shooter was not so merciful. The gods have their reasons, which we cannot know. Perhaps the god was too busy to help a small landholder and his wife, in humble Daulis.

At last, before spring came, the slaves and I laid out Strepsiades on his bier. The fever had consumed his fat and muscle; only skin and bone went into the grave. We buried him in the family plot, beside his parents and my poor dead child. I cried, with Kinesias, pouring libations of milk and oil, wine and water, onto my husband's new-dug grave. At least he would not be lonely there, and he would never cough again.

Chapter Twenty-two—Harmonia, The Slave

NANNO LOOKED UP AT PAUSON, her brown eyes wide, her lashes long and dark. "Would you like some lunch, husband? Or maybe just a cup of wine?"

He nodded. "Some of those grapes, and a cup of watered wine." He walked towards their bedroom, and she followed, signaling to Ktema and me to bring what he'd asked.

Philinna called to Nanno's slaves to follow her upstairs, back to the workroom. If they worked hard, the chiton would be finished by sunset.

In the cool of the kitchen, Ktema smiled as she dipped a cup of wine out of the amphora. "It's three months since her last period," she said. "She's been sick in the mornings, lately, too."

"I'd noticed," I said, putting deep purple grapes onto Pauson's favorite plate, the Pythia one. "And her belly's starting to swell. You can see it in that chiton she's got on today, if you look carefully."

Ktema grinned, and poured half the cup of wine onto the kitchen hearth, as a libation. "Artemis, twin of Apollo, protector of women, send her a strong boy."

Chapter Twenty-three—Thrasulla, The Priestess

ONCE MORE, I STOOD AT DAWN between the columns of Apollo's temple, and their wise counsel: "know yourself" and "nothing in excess." I waited there with Diodora and Kleitagora for the preliminary sacrifice, to see if Apollo would prophesy through us that day. If Perialla had truly known herself, if she had moderated her desires, she would have been standing there with us—not weighed down with gold, but honored by the god and all who served him. As for Kleomenes, I cannot say. His ways were strange, even to me.

The statue of Apollo Lukeios, the bronze wolf by the great altar, gleamed in the hazy autumn light. All over Phokis, farmers up before dawn were burning the detritus from their summer crops, the stems and withered leaves. The breeze was harsh with fire, but cold as ice, blowing down from the peak of pale, stony Parnassos. I shivered to see the white goat doused in cold water by Apollo's white-clothed priests, all of them garlanded with bay laurel. It shook with cold; the priests were satisfied. The god was ready. The goat would be sacrificed before us; soon, I would feel Apollo Lukeios within me, a ravening and merciless wolf.

I can't deny that Kleomenes' death was bloody and bizarre. Perhaps it was a god punishing him; few have offended so many powerful deities so blatantly in one short life. No one has asked the question of the oracle; until they do, I will not know the truth.

Until that time, I'm certain of one thing: Apollo Far-shooter, whose arrows bring disease, was not the god who killed the Spartan king. Kleomenes' strange death was mercifully quick. My husband's long, slow death, decades before, was far more terrible.

The sacrifice over, I followed the priests into the temple, ready to descend into Apollo's *adyton*, ready to speak for the god.

Further Reading

THE BEST WAY to understand the fifth century BC Greek world is to read the works of the world's greatest historians (Herodotus and Thucydides), tragic poets (Aeschylus, Sophocles and Euripides) and comic poets (Aristophanes and Menander). Homer's *Iliad* and *Odyssey*, though they were written several centuries earlier than the time of the novel and some of the material dates back to the Bronze Age, were the basis of an ancient Greek education and pervaded the consciousness of the classical Greeks.

Although he lived when the wars between Athens and Sparta were long over, Plutarch was a priest of Apollo at Delphi, and his writings on the oracle are indispensable. Pausanias' *Guide to Greece*, a second century AD version of a Lonely Planet guidebook, is a treasure-trove of religious and cultural data. If you can get hold of a copy, Sir JG Frazer's commentary on Pausanias is a masterpiece of erudition.

Life is too short to list the many excellent books I consulted while researching *The Priestess and the Slave*, but some stand out. *The Oxford Classical Dictionary* is a book for browsing in, rather than reading straight, but it is invaluable to anyone with an interest in the Classical world. Andrew Dalby's *Siren Feasts* is an accessible but detailed history of food in Greece. Hilary Deighton's *A Day in the Life of Ancient Athens* gives a lively overview of everyday life, and Robin Waterfield's *Athens: A History* is a masterly synthesis of Athenian history and culture. The scholarly works of Martin P. Nilsson and Walter Burkert bring out the strangeness of Greek religion, and its pervasive nature in the lives of the ancient Greeks.

About the Author

Author Photograph Russell Blackford

JENNY BLACKFORD was born in Sydney, Australia, and lives in Melbourne. She has always been fascinated by prehistory and ancient history, archaeology, ancient languages and mythology.

She studied Classics (Greek and Latin) at the University of Newcastle, NSW, including a year of German and Sanskrit as well as four years of Greek and Latin language, literature and history; she was awarded First Class Honors and a University Medal. Her postgraduate study in ancient religion was rendered discouraging by the shrinkage of Classics departments worldwide, and an ad in the paper propelled her into an unexpected career in computer networking.

Since Jenny started writing full-time, her stories have appeared in places including Jack Dann's important HarperCollins anthology *Dreaming Again,* Random House's *30 Australian Ghost Stories for Children* and Hadley Rille Books' *Ruins Terra*. She is one of the judges for the World Fantasy Awards 2009. Her next project is a novel about Bronze Age princess Medea, granddaughter of the Sun.

The Cover Illustration

THE PEOPLE OF NAXOS gave a monumental statue of a sphinx to Apollo at Delphi around 560BC. It originally stood on a tall Ionic column next to the sacred way that ran from the entrance of Apollo's sanctuary on Mount Parnassos up to his temple there. The sphinx is now on display in the Delphi Archaeological Museum.

The cover illustration by Rachael Mayo shows the time-weathered but still magnificent sphinx against the rocky slopes of Mount Parnassos.

www.ingramcontent.com/pod-product-compliance
Lightning Source LLC
Chambersburg PA
CBHW030641130626
46552CB00002B/964